"The Nail"
and Other Stories

Pedro Antonio de Alarcón in Emilia Pardo Bazán's *Alarcón: estudio biográfico.* Photo by Michael A. Micinilio.

"The Nail" and Other Stories

by

Pedro Antonio de Alarcón

Translated from the Spanish by
Robert M. Fedorchek

Introduction by
Cyrus C. DeCoster

Lewisburg
Bucknell University Press
London: Associated University Presses

Associated University Presses
440 Forsgate Drive
Cranbury, NJ 08512

Associated University Presses
16 Barter Street
London WC1A 2AH, England

Associated University Presses
P.O. Box 338, Port Credit
Mississauga, Ontario
Canada L5G 4L8

The paper used in this publication meets the requirements of the American National Standard for Permanence of Paper for Printed Library Materials Z39.48–1984.

Library of Congress Cataloging-in-Publication Data

Alarcón, Pedro Antonio de, 1833–1891.
[Short stories. Selections. English]
The nail, and other stories / by Pedro Antonio de Alarcón ; translated from the Spanish by Robert M. Fedorchek ; introduction by Cyrus C. DeCoster.
p. cm.
Contents: The nail—The cornet—The orderly—The foreigner—The French sympathizer—Long live the Pope!—The Mayor of Lapeza—The Guardian Angel.
Includes bibliographical references (p.).
ISBN 0-8387-5361-2 (alk. paper)
1. Alarcón, Pedro Antonio de, 1833–1891—Translations. I. Fedorchek, Robert M., 1938– . II. Title.
PQ6502.A24 1997
863′.5—dc21

97-2143
CIP

PRINTED IN THE UNITED STATES OF AMERICA

For Jack—brother, mentor, and friend.

Contents

Translator's Preface

PEDRO Antonio de Alarcón's *The Three-Cornered Hat* continues to be read with pleasure and delight more than a hundred years after its initial appearance in 1874, and few are the contemporary Spanish publishers that have not issued an edition of this masterpiece. It inspired Manuel de Falla's well-known ballet of the same title, and perhaps, as Ian Gibson suggests in *Federico García Lorca: A Life* (New York: Pantheon, 1989), aspects of Lorca's *The Shoemaker's Prodigious Wife*. Alarcón's contemporary Emilia Pardo Bazán pronounced it the "king of Spanish tales," and it has been as enduringly popular as José Zorrilla's *Don Juan Tenorio* and Juan Ramón Jiménez's *Platero and I*. *The Three-Cornered Hat* has received such acclaim because it represents the culmination of Alarcón's gift as a natural-born storyteller. But this masterpiece did not just appear out of nowhere; its harmony, near perfect structure, humor, irony, characterization, and movement resulted from the labors of a practitioner honing his craft.

During an especially productive decade, from 1853 to 1859, Alarcón published eight tales which would in time secure him a reputation as a first-rate storyteller—"The Nail" (1853), the two inspired by the first Carlist War, "The Cornet" (1854) and "The Orderly" (1854), and the five inspired by the War of Independence, "The Foreigner" (1854), "The French Sympathizer" (1856), "Long Live the Pope!" (1857), "The Mayor of Lapeza" (1859), and "The Guardian Angel" (1859).

The nail in "The Nail" is found driven through a disinterred skull, and if some of the events are implausible and others incredible, like a story that has gotten away from itself, it is also true that there is considerable suspense and mystery. Joan Estruch has observed in *Cuentos [de Alarcón]* (Barcelona: Ediciones Vicens-Vives, 1991) that "The Nail" is the first example of a detective story in Spanish literature. The extremes in both the heroine—three women in one—and the plot, inspired by *Le clou* of Hippolyte Lucas, make for a rebirth of Romanticism in mid-nineteenth century. And Laura de los Ríos, writing about the role of fate and the French source of "The Nail" in *La comendadora, El clavo y otros cuentos* (Madrid: Ediciones Cátedra, 1975) states that "the *cause célèbre* of French origin has been transformed into a good Spanish short story that leaves an unforgettable impression." An impression of love, passion, melodrama, and chance.

Of the two Carlist War tales "The Cornet" draws more heavily on historical reality with its depiction of the horror of civil war (friend against friend) and factual detail (shooting of hostages). Noteworthy for its first-person narration and rapid-fire dialogue, "The Cornet" paints an episode of fraternal love and the power of the will. "The Orderly," although set against the same Carlist War background, has more to do with a military "attitude" than a Carlist "War," and describes the transformation effected in one officer by one orderly.

The War of Independence stories have been known to generation after generation of Spanish readers, especially—for their theme of patriotism—"The French Sympathizer" and "The Mayor of Lapeza." These two, together with "Long Live the Pope!" and "The Guardian Angel," extol the heroism and courage of the Spanish people. The War of Independence (1808–1814) was fought against Napoleon and his attempt to place his brother Joseph on the Spanish throne, and after years of horrendous carnage and the Duke of Wellington's victory at Vitoria in 1813, the "Little Corporal" renounced the Spanish crown by the Treaty of Fontainebleau in 1814. "The Foreigner," the story of a young Pole who had been conscripted into Napoleon's army, looks at Spain and two of her soldiers through the eyes of a Spanish muleteer.

"The Nail" has been translated into English several times, but the most readily available versions (see the Select Bibliography) are not at all faithful to Alarcón's text, and the translators have broken a cardinal rule of translation—adding passages of their own while at the same time excising Alarcón's original sentences.

The two Carlist War and five War of Independence stories are here brought together in English translation for the first time in one book. Along with "The Nail" they constitute an impressive collection of eight stories published by Alarcón in the space of a half dozen years.

Words and passages marked with an asterisk (*) in the text are explained in the Notes at the back of the book.

Finally, a word of thanks. Only with effort can I imagine a translator who has been assisted over the years more willingly and been served more faithfully than I have by my *compadre,* friend, and colleague of thirty-six years, Pedro S. Rivas Díaz, *esclarecido hijo de Puerto Rico y distinguido nieto de España.*

Pedro Antonio de Alarcón in Julio Romano's *Pedro Antonio de Alarcón: el novelista romántico*. Photo by Robert M. Fedorchek.

Caricature of Pedro Antonio de Alarcón by Angel Pons on the cover of the 13 October 1888 issue of *Los Madriles*. Photo by Robert M. Fedorchek. Courtesy, Hemeroteca Municipal, Madrid.

Second of May 1808, engraving by José Ribelles: the uprising of the people of Madrid at the Puerta del Sol against Napoleon's troops. It marked the beginning of Spain's War of Independence, which inspired five of Alarcón's short stories. Photo by Robert M. Fedorchek.

Francisco de Goya's "Executions of the Third of May 1808" on a mosaic of ceramic tile. This monument stands in the very small, narrow Cementerio de la Florida of Madrid, on Calle de Francisco y Jacinto Alcántara, 2, that contains the remains of forty-three of the Spaniards executed on that date. This cemetery, alongside Madrid's Escuela Municipal de Cerámica, is opened only two days of the year: May 2 and 3. Photo by Robert M. Fedorchek.

Francisco de Goya's "El 3 de mayo de 1808: los fusilamientos de la montaña del Príncipe Pío" (Executions of the Third of May 1808 at the Príncipe Pío Mountain), in Madrid's Prado Museum. Photo by Robert M. Fedorchek.

Introduction

Cyrus C. DeCoster

PEDRO Antonio de Alarcón was born in 1833 in Guadix, then an impoverished city of ten thousand inhabitants in the foothills of the Sierra Nevada forty miles east of Granada. He studied law for a few months at the University of Granada, but his parents could ill afford the cost. He then enrolled in the seminary in Guadix but found that he had little calling for the clergy. Writing was what really attracted him, and he began a historical drama, *La conquista de Guadix (The Conquest of Guadix),* which has been lost, and an early version of the novel *El final de Norma (Norma's End)*. In 1852 with his friend Torcuato Tárrago, who was later to write countless mediocre historical novels, he found a wealthy sponsor to subsidize *El Eco de Occidente,* a weekly literary journal published in Cádiz. Here appeared some of his first stories, including "El clavo (The Nail)." In 1854 he moved to Granada taking *El Eco* with him. He found the intellectual climate there congenial, associating with a group of young writers and artists who came to be known as the *Cuerda granadina (Granada Chain)*. They were so christened when one evening a group of them entered the theater holding on to each other to keep their balance as the aisles were narrow, and someone cried out: "¡Ahí va la cuerda!" (There goes the chain of galley slaves.) They were young and high-spirited, typical of the post-Romantic era in the lighthearted attitude they adopted toward life, art, and literature.

In the fall of 1854 Alarcón moved to Madrid, several of his Granada friends joining him there, and the *Cuerda granadina* became the *Colonia granadina*. They added some new recruits, including Antonio de Trueba, Agustín Bonnat, Núñez de Arce, and Mariano de Larra, the son of the essayist. The same carefree, bohemian attitude continued to prevail.

But it was politics rather than literature that absorbed Alarcón during this time. In December of 1854 he began writing for the new democratic newspaper *El Látigo* and the following month he took over the editorship. He attacked the standard villains of the liberals, Narváez and María Cristina, the Queen Mother, and protested against taxes, conscription, graft, and capital punishment. His tone is irreverent, almost sacrilegious, as when he paraphrases the Beatitudes, the Creed, and even the Lord's Prayer to dramatize abuses in the government. His pungently bitter satire reminds one of Larra. This Alarcón has nothing in common with the apologist who twenty years later wrote *El escándalo (The Scandal)*. Alarcón became embroiled in a polemic with the Venezuelan Heriberto García de Quevedo, who was writing for the conservative paper *El León Español*. Alarcón insulted his adversary and was challenged to a duel. A novice with firearms, he fired first and missed. García de Quevedo, an experienced duelist, magnanimously fired into the air. Alarcón was badly shaken by the experience. He resigned from *El Látigo*, resolved never again to take part in politics, and went off to Segovia for a month to lick his wounds.

Except for occasional brief trips, Alarcón spent the next five years, until he left for Africa in late 1859, in Madrid. His horizons had broadened and he had access to the best periodicals. The reworked manuscript of *El final de Norma* was published in the paper *El Occidente* in the fall of 1855. It is impossibly melodramatic by today's tastes, but it was popular in its day and was reprinted many times. He continued to cultivate the short story assiduously. Two-thirds of his total production, including all the stories in this collection, are from these years. In addition, he published many articles of literary criticism and *costumbrista* sketches. When Spain declared war on Morocco in October of 1859, Alarcón went as a war correspondent. His jingoistic reports were enthusiastically received by the Spanish public. After returning to Madrid late in March, he collected them in the two-volume *Diario de un testigo de la Guerra de Africa (Diary of a Witness to the African War)*. He had acquired a measure of fame, and, more tangibly, he was now financially comfortably off.

During the next decade Alarcón largely neglected literature and again turned his attention to politics, although our fiery liberal had become conservative. He was elected deputy from Guadix and was reelected regularly to the Cortes [Spanish Parliament] until defeated in 1872. He also served briefly as Councilor of State in the Department of Public Works, the highest political office he was to hold. His role, however, in the political life of Spain was minor.

Then, in the seventies, writing again became his primary interest.

Early in the decade he brought out collections of short pieces which had previously appeared in periodicals, *Poesías serias y humorísticas (Serious and Humorous Poetry),* 1870, and *Cosas que fueron (Things of the Past),* 1871, consisting of *costumbrista* sketches. In 1872 he spent ten days traveling by horseback through the Alpujarra, the southern part of the province of Granada lying between the Sierra Nevada and the Mediterranean, then a very inaccessible part of Spain. Much of it was even closed to wheeled traffic. The last Moorish resistance was centered there. His account of the trip, *La Alpujarra,* came out two years later. He describes the changing countryside, the magnificent mountain panoramas, the picturesque villages, and the people he meets, but over half the book is devoted to evoking the tragic conflict between the Christians and the Moors that led to the expulsion of the latter. Historical passages alternate with narrative and descriptive ones throughout the book so the reader is constantly associating the beautiful country with its calamitous history. It is one of the most interesting travel books written in Spain in the nineteenth century.

The novel was a relatively neglected genre in Spain during most of the nineteenth century. Fernán Caballero, a transitional figure during the middle years of the century, author of *La gaviota (The Sea Gull), Clemencia,* and *La familia de Alvareda (The Alvareda Family),* was the leading novelist bridging the gap between Romanticism and Realism. Her novels are of interest historically, but they are little read today. Important novels started to appear in the seventies. Alarcón reached the age of forty before he set out to make a name for himself as a novelist. *El final de Norma* would be forgotten today if he were not the author. His contemporaries were also slow in trying their hand at what was to become the major genre of the century. Valera was fifty when he wrote *Pepita Jiménez* and Pereda forty-three when *El buey suelto (The Bachelor)* appeared in 1877. The delay is understandable, for the renascence of the novel was in part a product of the greater stability brought about by the Restoration, the ascent of Alfonso XII to the throne in 1875.

During a seven-year period, Alarcón published his five significant novels: the delightfully comic *El sombrero de tres picos (The Three-Cornered Hat)* in 1874, the three ideological novels with a conservative bent, *El escándalo* in 1875, *El Niño de la bola (The Infant with the Globe)* in 1880, *La pródiga (The Prodigal Woman)* in 1882, and *El Capitán Veneno (Captain Poison),* a charming love story, in 1881.

The story of *The Three-Cornered Hat* is so well-known that it scarcely requires retelling. It is a tale of attempted double seduction. The lecherous Corregidor, or chief magistrate, tries to seduce the miller's wife and he, in turn, to gain revenge, does the same with the Corregidora, the magistrate's wife. Both men are unsuccessful and the novel ends with the miller and his wife happily united and the Corregidora banishing her husband from her bedroom for life. The tale forms part of the Western European folkloric tradition. Other versions end less innocently with a double seduction and the two couples amicably having breakfast together the following morning. Alarcón portrays the backwardness of the country and the all-too-prevalent abuses in an ironical tone suggestive of Valera. It lends a charming humor to the novel that is seldom found in his longer, more ponderous ones. It met with instantaneous success when first published and its popularity has continued unabated to this day.

El Capitán Veneno is a short, sentimental story which is told with engaging humor. It is a reversal of the traditional story of *The Taming of the Shrew.* This time it is the intractable male who is brought to terms. It is a pleasant, lightweight novel that has been largely ignored by the critics.

During the 1870s, with the greater freedom that came with the Restoration, religion began to receive a lot of outspoken scrutiny in the Spanish novel. The anticlerical bias was unmistakable in Galdós's so-called unholy trinity, *Doña Perfecta, Gloria,* and *La familia de León Roch (The Family of León Roch).* Alarcón's *El escándalo* was the most vociferous answer of the conservatives and Neo-Catholics to this challenge. It is the story of the exemplary conversion and reformation of a young rake. Alarcón makes his didactic message abundantly clear. One can understand how the readers were polarized by the novel. The ultramontane conservatives found it inspirational; the liberals, overdrawn and unduly pious.

After *El final de Norma, El Niño de la bola,* who is the patron saint of the town, is the most romantic of Alarcón's novels. *El escándalo* is above all a didactic work; the romantic influence is seen mainly in the fortuitous twists of the plot. In *El Niño de la bola,* on the other hand, the passionate love story, which ends with the violent deaths of the two protagonists, is all important. Ideology plays a secondary role. Montesinos went so far as to say: "Our best romantic novel is possibly *El Niño de la bola.*"

The woman of easy virtue seen from different vantage points is a recurring theme in European literature of the nineteenth century: Dumas's *La Dame aux Camélias (Camille),* Zola's infamous *Nana,*

Galdós's *La desheredada (The Disinherited Lady),* Daudet's *Sapho,* Valera's *Genio y figura (Rafaela),* and *La pródiga* all are variations of this theme. In *La pródiga* a woman commits suicide to spare her lover unhappiness. It is the most tightly constructed of Alarcón's novels. The only part which rings false is the melodramatic account of her early dissolute life with a series of affairs that all end disastrously. The plot moves quickly to the final resolution with no abrupt reversals in the action. The didactic bias is also less pronounced than in *El escándalo.* Perhaps the critics have paid insufficient attention to it.

El escándalo and *El Niño de la bola* had both been coolly received by the major critics, Revilla, Clarín, Palacio Valdés, and Antonio de Valbuena, while, by and large, they had little to say about *El Capitán Veneno* and *La pródiga.* Alarcón was hurt and discouraged, and he wrote little during the last decade of his life. His last book was the autobiographical *Historia de mis libros (The History of My Books),* 1884. He was also seriously overweight and in poor health. He suffered a series of strokes and died in 1891 at the age of fifty-eight.

Alarcón wrote some forty short stories, the majority of them during the 1850's when he was in his twenties. Then he became involved in politics and in the seventies he focused his attention on the novel. During these twenty years he produced fewer than a dozen stories.

In his *Historia de mis libros,* Alarcón divides his short stories chronologically into three groups. The early ones, written in Guadix and Granada, show the influence of the Romantics, Scott, Dumas, and Hugo. The second group comprises the stories he wrote after coming to Madrid in 1854 when he was under the influence of the French humorist Alphonse Karr and his Spanish disciple, Agustín Bonnat. Bonnat published humorous, fantastic stories in the journals of the time, but is today virtually forgotten. It was his mannered, exaggerated style, in particular, that Alarcón imitated. In retrospect, he looks back on this fad of his as an aberration, and he characterizes many of the stories of this period as extravagant and buffoonish. In the final group, he has renounced his "Bonnat" manner. These late stories, the work of the mature Alarcón, are consistently of superior quality.

Alarcón began to publish his so-called *Obras completas* in the "Colección de Escritores Castellanos" in 1881. The short stories were grouped in three volumes according to thematic material,

Cuentos amatorios (1881), *Historietas nacionales* (1881), and *Narraciones inverosímiles* (1882). How is the word *inverosímiles* in the third title to be interpreted? It is usually translated as improbable, unlikely. Montesinos thinks Alarcón chose the title because the stories, unlike most of those in the other two volumes, are invented, not based on actual events as are many of the stories in *Historietas nacionales*. Alarcón corroborates in *Historia de mis libros* that almost without exception they were original conceptions, "pura química de mi imaginación," pure products of my imagination.

Robert Fedorchek has translated eight of the early stories, all written between 1853 and 1859. "The Nail," "The Cornet," "The Orderly," and "The Foreigner" first appeared in *El Eco de Occidente* in 1854; and the first two were reprinted in the *Semanario Pintoresco Español* in 1855. "The French Sympathizer," "Long Live the Pope!," "The Mayor of Lapeza," and "The Guardian Angel" came out in *El Museo Universal* in the late 1850s. "The Nail" was subsequently collected in Alarcón's *Cuentos amatorios,* and the other seven, all of them war stories, in the *Historietas nacionales*. Two, "The Cornet" and "The Orderly," deal with the Carlist War, the other five with the War of Independence. In "The Mayor of Lapeza" and "The French Sympathizer," probably his two most popular stories, Alarcón glorifies the bravery of the Spaniards in their struggle against Napoleon. The chauvinistic tone, the improbably heroic exploits of the Spaniards, the barbarous deeds of the invaders, and the exaggeratedly rhetorical language are indications of their romantic affiliation. The protagonist of "The Mayor of Lapeza," the mayor of a village of charcoal makers near Guadix, heads the heroic if futile defense of the town by the vastly outnumbered peasants against a French army. At the end, surrounded and seriously wounded, he hurls himself to death on the rocks below the town to avoid being captured. In "The French Sympathizer," an apothecary is accused of being a French sympathizer for consorting with the enemy. One evening while he is hosting a banquet for twenty French officers, the townspeople break in, intent on killing him for his treachery. Instead, they find that he has poisoned the wine, and both he and the officers are about to expire. The final scene, with the townspeople supporting the hero surrounded by dead and dying Frenchmen, could scarcely be more melodramatic.

Other stories have a different slant. "The Guardian Angel" is an inadvertent tragedy. A mother takes refuge from the French with her baby in a dry cistern. When the baby starts to cry, she clutches him to her breast so the pursuing soldiers will not hear him. She is saved, but the baby suffocates, and she subsequently loses her mind. In "The Foreigner" the villain is a Spanish soldier who cold-bloodedly kills and robs a sick Polish prisoner named Iwa near Almería. Some years later he is taken prisoner and is forced to join Napoleon's army invading Russia. He falls ill in Warsaw and is cared for by a Polish family, but the mother recognizes the locket he is wearing as one that had belonged to her son Iwa. She and her daughters, to gain revenge, brutally claw him to death. The jingoistic tone of the other war stories is absent, but the romantic strain is still strong. It is a violent tale, and the outcome depends heavily on coincidence. Alarcón's pro-Catholic leanings are very evident in "Long Live the Pope!" Some Spanish prisoners who are being marched across France show exaggerated respect and affection for the Pope, who under Napoleon's orders is being driven into exile in Paris.

"The Nail," from *Cuentos amatorios,* is one of the longest and most popular of Alarcón's stories, over half the length of *El Capitán Veneno*. It is understandable that mid-nineteenth century readers should be carried away by the sensational and melodramatic plot, but it is full of improbabilities and the conclusion is difficult to accept. A judge has sentenced to death the woman he loves for having murdered her husband. He comes galloping up with the pardon just as she is being led to the gallows, but at that very moment she dies, overcome by emotion.

"The Nail" is the only story in this collection which contains examples of Alarcón's "Bonnat" manner. It begins with a waggish note, a prologue consisting of a single sentence: "Felipe (the narrator and a good friend of the judge) lighted a cigar and spoke as follows." Then follows the phrase: "End of the prologue." Alarcón entitles the first chapter: "Number I." Nothing more. Then the narrator meets a beautiful woman on a stagecoach and wonders: "And her sadness? *Quare causa?*" The Italian phrase adds an incongruous note to his curiosity. Alarcón inserts obscure allusions which only obfuscate the situation. The narrator wished that it would storm so that he could see his companion: "And so I asked heaven to send lightning flashes, like Gertrudis Gómez de Avellaneda's Alfonso Munio when he exclaims: 'Dreadful storm, send me a thunderbolt!'" Alfonso Munio was the protagonist of La Avellaneda's historical play of the same name. Shortly afterwards, Felipe succeeds in ingratiating himself with his companion and she recounts to him "a number of other doleful generalities à la Balzac." Neither reference seems relevant in the context. Sometime later, the narrator again meets a mysterious woman at a soirée in Granada. The title of the chapter, "A duet in E major," would seem to suggest that something is brewing between them, but they take leave of each other and nothing happens. It later turns out that the three women are one and the same—the mysterious woman in the stagecoach whom the narrator never gets to see, the one he encounters at the soirée, and the judge's great love, who dies on the scaffold. Other stories such as "The Embrace at Vergara" and "April and May Mornings" from *Cuentos amatorios* and "The Six Veils" from *Narraciones inverosímiles* also have many "Bonnat" touches.

Fedorchek has given us a selection of Alarcón's most typical and popular stories from the early years. Several of them have been translated before, but the nineteenth-century translations of Spanish fiction are frequently infelicitous and sometimes incorrect; and people who don't read Spanish will be pleased to have these accurate and smooth-reading versions available.

During the 1850s, with his *Historietas nacionales* steeped in the post-romantic tradition, Alarcón was the leading writer of short stories in Spain. Fernán Caballero was his closest competitor. Later on, despite his involvement in politics and novel writing, he also managed to produce some superior stories. Among his contemporaries, Valera occasionally tried his hand at the short story, and he did write two of the best Spanish stories of the century, "The Green Bird" and "Parsondes." Pereda is known above all for his *costumbrista* novels and sketches, not his short stories, while Bécquer with his romantic *Legends* stands somewhat apart from the others. In the closing years of the century, Galdós, Clarín, and particularly Pardo Bazán dominated the short story and turned it into new channels with their emphasis on the realistic portrayal of bourgeois society and the psychological analysis of the characters.

“The Nail” and Other Stories

El clavo

The Nail
Cause Célèbre

PROLOGUE

Felipe lighted a cigar and spoke as follows:

END OF PROLOGUE

I
NUMBER 1

The thing most ardently desired by every man who climbs aboard a diligence to embark on a long journey is that luck bring him traveling companions who converse pleasantly, have the same tastes and same vices, few impertinent qualities, good manners, and an openness which does not lapse into familiarity.

Because, as has been said and demonstrated by Larra, Kock, Soulié,* and other writers of customs, such an improvised and close gathering of two or more persons is a serious matter indeed. They have never seen each other, and most likely will not see each other ever again, but nevertheless they are destined, through a stroke of fate, to rub shoulders, to have breakfast, lunch, and dinner together, to sleep on top of one another—in short, to treat one another with an abandon and intimacy that we withhold even from our closest friends, that is, with the habits and failings confined to home and family.

When you open the door, turbulent fears seize the imagination: an old woman with asthma, a smoker of foul tobacco, an ugly woman who cannot tolerate the smoke of the aromatic variety, a wet nurse who suffers from motion sickness, angelic children who fuss and cry, a grave man who snores, a venerable matron who takes up a seat and a half, an Englishman who does not speak Spanish (I assume that you do not speak English)—such are, among others, the types you are afraid to encounter.

Now and then you cherish the sweet hope of running across a beautiful traveling companion, a widow of twenty or thirty (even thirty-six), for example, with whom to share the inconveniences of the trip, but as soon as such a pleasant thought occurs to you, you hasten to dispel it with a long face, considering that a like adventure would be excessive for a simple mortal in this valley of tears and absurdities.

Preoccupied with similar anxieties, I climbed into the closed forward compartment of the Granada-Málaga diligence at five minutes to eleven on a fall night in 1844, a dark, stormy night, to be exact.

As I settled inside with ticket number 2 in my pocket, my first consideration was to greet the unknown holder of number 1 who was causing me so much concern even before we met.

It should be observed that the third seat in the compartment was not taken, according to the head coachman.

"Good evening," I said as soon as I sat down, directing my voice toward the corner where I expected my close-quarters companion to be.

A silence as profound as the prevailing darkness followed my "Good evening."

«The devil!» I thought. «I wonder if he or she, my epicene companion, is deaf.»

And in a louder voice I repeated:

"Good evening!"

My second greeting met with the same silence.

«I wonder if he or she is dumb,» I then thought.

In the meantime, the diligence, drawn by ten spirited horses, had begun to roll, or rather, fly.

My bewilderment was growing.

With whom was I traveling? A man? A woman? If the latter, young or old? Just who was that silent number 1?

And, whoever it was, why was he keeping quiet? Why was he not returning my greeting? Could he have been intoxicated? Or have fallen asleep? Or have died? Could he have been a thief?

I needed a light but did not smoke then and had no matches with me.

What was I to do?

Such were my reflections when it occurred to me to call on the sense of touch since I was getting nowhere with those of sight and hearing.

With more care than a pickpocket takes to steal a handkerchief from us at the Puerta del Sol,* I extended my right hand toward the corner of the compartment.

My most fervent desire was to stumble upon a silk skirt, or a wool skirt, or even a percale skirt.

So I moved over.

Nothing.

I moved over further; I extended the length of my arm . . . nothing.

I moved again, and with my hand felt and probed both sides, then all four corners, under the seats, and the ceiling straps.

Nothing. Nothing at all.

At that moment there was a flash of lightning—I've already said it was a stormy night—and by its sulphurous light I saw that I was completely alone.

I burst into laughter, making fun of myself, and at that very instant the diligence stopped.

We had arrived at the first relay.

I was getting ready to ask the coachman about the missing passenger when the door opened, and, by the light of the station boy's lantern, I saw—I saw what I thought was a dream.

I saw climbing into the compartment with me a supremely beautiful woman—young, graceful, pale, alone, and dressed in mourning.

It was number 1, my erstwhile epicene traveling companion, the widow of my hopes, the fulfillment of the dream that I hadn't dared to entertain; it was the *ne plus ultra* of my illusions as a traveler; it was she!

I mean it was to *be* she with time.

II

SKIRMISHES

As soon as I gave the unknown woman my hand to help her inside, she sat down next to me, murmuring a "Thank you" and "Good evening" that touched my heart, and the following regrettable and distressing thought occurred to me:

«It's only fifty-five miles from here to Málaga. If only we were going to the Kamchatka Peninsula!»*

In the meantime, the door was closed and we were left in the dark.

This meant that I could not see her.

And so I asked heaven to send lightning flashes, like Gertrudis Gómez de Avellaneda's Alfonso Munio when he exclaims:

Dreadful storm, send me a thunderbolt!*

But, oh, affliction, the storm was already moving southward.

And not seeing her was not the worst thing—the worst thing was that the elegant lady's severe, downcast air had intimidated me to such an extent that I didn't dare do anything.

However, after several minutes I asked the usual questions and made the usual observations which, little by little, establish a certain intimacy among travelers:

"Are you all right?"

"Are you going to Málaga?"

"Did you like the Alhambra?"

"Are you coming from Granada?"

"It's a damp night."

To which she responded:

"Fine, thank you."

"Yes."

"No, sir."

"Oh!"

"Indeed!"

My traveling companion had, to be sure, little desire to engage in conversation.

I determined, therefore, to come up with better questions, but seeing that none occurred to me I began to reflect.

Why had that woman gotten on at the first relay station and not in Granada?

Why was she alone?

Was she married?

Was she a widow?

Was she . . . ?

And her sadness? *Quare causa?* What was behind it?

I couldn't get any answers to these questions without being indiscreet, and I liked the traveler too much to run the risk of striking her as a common man who asked foolish things.

How I wished dawn would break!

During the day people speak with justifiable freedom, while in the dark conversation is almost like touching—it goes straight to the point, it's a betrayal of trust.

From her breathing and occasional sighs, I gathered that the unknown woman did not sleep a wink all night.

And I think it's unnecessary to say that I didn't sleep either.

"Are you indisposed?" I asked her one of the times that she groaned.

"No, sir, thank you. Please. Sleep and do not be troubled on my account."

"Sleep!" I exclaimed.

Then I added:

"I thought you were unwell."

"Oh, no, I'm not unwell," she murmured softly, but in a tone that betrayed a certain bitterness.

During the rest of the night her conversation consisted only of laconic exchanges, like the preceding one.

Dawn broke at last.

How beautiful she was!

But what grief was knitted on her brow! What dreadful gloom emanated from her lovely eyes! What a tragic expression stamped the whole of her face! There had to be something very sorrowful in the depths of her soul.

However, she was not one of those extravagant, exceptional women of a romantic stripe who live removed from the world, suffering some sort of distress or performing in some sort of tragedy.

She was a fashionable, elegant woman with a distinguished air, a woman whose least utterance revealed one of those queens of conversation and good taste who have for a throne an armchair in their boudoir, a coach at the Prado or a box at the opera, but who fall silent outside of their element, that is, outside the circle of their equals.

With the light of day my charming travel companion cheered up somewhat, and whether my circumspection during the night and the seriousness of my expression spoke well of me, or whether she wished to recompense the man whom she had kept from sleeping, she then touched on the prescribed topics:

"Where are you going?"

"It's going to be a lovely day."

"What gorgeous scenery!'

To which I responded more extensively than she did earlier.

We had breakfast in Colmenar.

Neither the forward nor the rear passengers were very friendly and my traveling companion confined herself to talking to me.

Needless to say I was completely devoted to her and waited on her at table as if she were royalty.

Back in the diligence we treated one another with somewhat more familiarity.

Over the meal we had spoken about Madrid, and to speak well of Madrid to a lady who comes from the capital and is far away from it is the best of recommendations. Because nothing is as captivating as Madrid left behind.

«Now or never, Felipe!» I then said to myself. «Another twenty-five miles. Let's broach the love issue.»

III
Catastrophe

Poor me! No sooner did I speak gallant words to my beauty than I realized I had raised a sore subject.

I immediately lost all the favor I had gained in her eyes.

She communicated that to me with an indefinable look that brought me up short.

"Thank you, kind sir, thank you," she said to me after a moment when she saw that I was changing the topic of conversation.

"Have I upset you, madam?"

"Yes. Love horrifies me. How sad it is to inspire what one does not feel! What I would give not to attract anyone!"

"It's necessary for you to do something, unless you take pleasure in somebody else's suffering," I responded very seriously. "The proof is that you've made me regret meeting you. If not happily, yesterday at least I lived peacefully, and now I'm miserable, inasmuch as I love you and there is no hope."

"You can take satisfaction on one score, my friend," she said, smiling.

"What?"

"If I reject your love, it's not because it's yours, but because it's love. So you can be certain that not today, not tomorrow, not ever, will I return another man's love. I'll never love anyone again."

"But why, madam?"

"Because my heart refuses, because it cannot, because it should not struggle any longer. Because I have loved to the point of delirium, and I have been deceived. In short, because I abhor love."

Magnificent speech! I was not enamored of that woman. She inspired me with curiosity and desire on account of her refinement and beauty, but it was still a long way from there to passion.

And so, upon hearing those painful and categorical words, my manly heart gave up the struggle and my artistic imagination came into play. By this I mean that I began to speak to the unknown lady a moral, philosophical language that was in the best of tastes, and with it I succeeded in regaining her trust—that is, she related to me a number of other doleful generalities à la Balzac.

Thus did we arrive in Málaga.

It was the most opportune moment to learn the name of that most unusual woman.

While saying goodbye to her at the station, I told her my name, where I would be staying, and my address in Madrid.

She responded in a tone of voice that I will never forget:

"I thank you from the bottom of my heart for the many kindnesses that you showed me during our trip, and I ask you to forgive me if I withhold my name instead of giving you a false one, which is how I appear on the passenger list."

"Oh!" I exclaimed. "Then, we will never see each other again."

"Never—which should not distress you."

And so saying, she gave me a joyless smile, extended her hand to me with exquisite grace, and murmured:

"Pray to God for me."

I shook her lovely, delicate hand and with a bow ended our farewell, which was beginning to upset me rather considerably.

At this point a luxurious carriage arrived at the hostelry.

A footman in a black uniform beckoned to the unknown lady.

She got inside, waved goodbye, and disappeared in the direction of Puerta del Mar.

* * *

Two months later I ran across her again.

Let's see where.

IV

Another Journey

At two o'clock in the afternoon on November 1st of that year I was riding an old post horse along the stone-paved road that leads to____, an important municipality and administrative center of the province of Córdoba.

My servant and luggage were on another and much worse horse.

I was traveling to ____ with the idea of leasing some land and spending three or four weeks at the home of the lower-court judge, a very good friend whom I had met at the University of Granada when both of us were studying jurisprudence. Although we had developed a close friendship and become inseparable, afterwards we hadn't seen each other for seven years.

The more I neared the town that was the object of my journey, the more I distinctly heard the gloomy knell of numerous bells that were tolling for the dead.

I was not at all amused by such a lugubrious coincidence.

Nevertheless, there was nothing fortuitous about that tolling and I should have expected it, seeing that it was the day before All Souls' Day.

Anyway, I reached, in a very bad mood, the open arms of my friend, who was waiting for me on the outskirts of the town.

He noticed my anxiety at once and, after we had exchanged greetings, asked about it.

"What's the matter?" he said, taking my arm as his servants and mine went on ahead with the horses.

"Well, I'll be frank," I replied, "I've never deserved nor do I intend to deserve to have arches of triumph erected for me. I've never experienced that immense joy which will fill the heart of a great man at the moment a jubilant town comes forth to receive him while bells are ringing, but—"

"Where's this going to end?"

"In the second part of my speech, which is that if in this town I have not experienced the honors of a triumphal entrance, I have just been the object of others which are very similar, although completely opposite. Admit, you ignorant judge, that those funeral knells that commemorate my arrival in ____ would have saddened the most jovial man in the world."

"Bravo, Felipe!" exclaimed the judge, whom we'll call Joaquín

Zarco. "This is very much to my liking. Your melancholy matches my sadness perfectly."

"You sad? Since when?"

Joaquín shrugged his shoulders, and not without effort suppressed a moan.

When two friends who truly love each other meet up after a long separation, it seems as though they resurrect all the sorrows which they have not wept over together.

I pretended not to notice for the moment and spoke to Zarco about inconsequential matters.

At this point we entered his luxurious home.

"The deuce, my friend!" I couldn't help exclaim. "What elegant furnishings! What order, what good taste in everything! How foolish of me. Now I get it. You're married."

"I haven't married," the judge responded in a somewhat disturbed tone of voice. "I haven't married and I never will."

"That you haven't married, I believe, since you didn't write to me about it. And that would have been worth telling. But saying you'll never marry doesn't seem as simple or believable to me."

"Well, I swear it!" Zarco replied solemnly.

"What an odd transformation!" I countered. "You've always been a staunch supporter of the seventh sacrament. You wrote to me two years ago advising me to get married and now you come out with this surprise? My friend, something has happened to you, something very painful."

"To me?" said Zarco, shuddering.

"To you!" I continued. "And you're going to tell me all about it. You live here alone, imprisoned in the grave circumspection required by your position, with no friend in whom to confide your human weaknesses. Well, tell me everything and let's see if I can be of any help to you."

The judge shook my hands, saying:

"Yes, yes. You'll hear it all, my friend. I'm terribly unfortunate!"

Then he calmed down a little and added dryly:

"Change clothes. Today the whole town is going to visit the cemetery and it would look bad if I weren't there. You'll come with me. It's a nice afternoon and you need to walk to rest from the trip on horseback. The cemetery is in the middle of a beautiful field and you'll enjoy the stroll. Along the way I'll tell you what has made my life miserable, and you'll see whether or not I have reason to detest women."

An hour later Zarco and I were walking toward the cemetery. My poor friend spoke to me as follows:

V
Recollections of a Lower-Court Judge

(1)

"***Two*** years ago, when I was a public prosecutor in ——, I obtained permission to spend a month in Seville.

"At the inn where I stayed there lived an elegant and very beautiful young woman. She had been there for several weeks and passed for a widow, but where she came from and what kept her in Seville was a mystery to the other boarders.

"Her solitude, her life of luxury, her lack of acquaintances, and the air of sadness that surrounded her gave rise to endless conjecture, all of which, added to her incomparable beauty and the inspiration and the pleasure with which she played the piano and sang, soon awakened in me an insuperable attraction for that woman.

"Her rooms were directly above mine, so that I heard her sing and play and come and go, and I even knew when she went to bed, when she got up, and when she had a sleepless night—which occurred quite frequently. Although she had her meals served in her room, instead of eating at the guest table, and never went to the theater, I had occasion to doff my hat to her a number of times, either on the stairs or in a shop or from balcony to balcony, and soon both of us were certain of the pleasure with which we saw each other.

"You know my character. I was serious, although not gloomy, and my circumspection suited that woman's secluded life perfectly. I never spoke a word to her, never attempted to visit her in her room, and never chased after her with annoying curiosity like other men lodgers at the inn.

"This respect for her melancholy must have flattered her pride as a patient, and I say so because in a very short time she began to look at me with a certain deference, as if we had already come to an understanding.

"A fortnight had gone by like this when fate, pure fate, ushered me into the unknown lady's apartment one night.

"As our rooms occupied the exact same location in the building, except on different floors, the entrances were identical. On the night in question, I was distracted as I returned from the theater and climbed more steps than I should have, and opened the door to her apartment thinking that it was the one to mine.

"The beauty was reading and gave a start when she saw me. I was so stunned that I could barely excuse myself, but my very embarrassment and the haste with which I tried to leave convinced her that my mistake was not a sham. So she retained me with exquisite kindness 'in order to demonstrate,' she said, 'that she believed in my good faith and that she wasn't angry with me,' and she ended up begging me to be mistaken again, deliberately, since she couldn't allow a person of my disposition to spend evenings on the balcony listening to her sing—'as she had seen me doing'—when 'her modest ability would be honored if I were closer.'

"In spite of all that she said, I considered it my duty not to stay that night and left.

"Three days went by, during which I still didn't dare take advantage of that lovely woman's kind offer, even at the risk of seeming rude in her eyes. And the fact is I was hopelessly in love with her; the fact is I understood that in a love affair with a woman like her there could be no halfway point, only the utmost heartache or the utmost happiness; and finally the fact is I feared the atmosphere of sadness that surrounded her.

"However, after those three days, I went up to the third floor.

"I spent the whole evening there. She told me that her name was Blanca, that she was a Madrilenian, and that she was a widow. She played the piano, sang, asked me a thousand questions about myself, my profession, my marital status, my family, etc., and every one of her words and observations gratified me and captivated me. From that night on my soul was a slave of hers.

"I visited her the following evening, and also the next evening, and afterwards every evening and every day.

"We loved each other, and not a word of love had passed between us.

"But, while discussing love, I had stressed to her the importance that I attached to it, the fervor of my ideas and passions, and all that my heart needed in order to be happy.

"For her part, she had stated to me that she felt the same way.

"'I married my husband without loving him,' she said one evening. 'A short time later . . . I hated him. He's dead now. Only God knows how much I've suffered. Here's how I understand love: it's heaven or it's hell. And for me, up to now, it has always been hell.'

"I didn't sleep that night.

"I lay awake dissecting Blanca's last words.

"How superstitious I was! That woman frightened me. Would I become her heaven and she my hell?

"In the meantime, my month's leave of absence was expiring.

"I could have asked for another one, using illness as an excuse, but—should I have?

"I consulted Blanca.

"'Why are you asking *me?*' she said, taking my hand.

"'The plain truth, Blanca,' I answered, 'is that I love you. Am I making a mistake loving you?'

"'No,' she said, turning pale.

"And flashes of light and sensuality shone in her black eyes."

(2)

"So I requested two months additional leave, which were granted to me thanks to you. If only you hadn't done me that favor!

"My relations with Blanca weren't love—they were delirium, madness, fanaticism.

"Far from my frenzy being moderated with the possession of that extraordinary woman, it continued to intensify. With each passing day I discovered new compatibilities between us, new treasures of happiness, new sources of contentment.

"But in my spirit, as in hers, mysterious fears were arising at the same time.

"We were afraid of losing each other, which was the reason for our anxiety.

"Ordinary love needs fear to feed itself, to not wane. That's why it's been said that every illicit relationship is more passionate than marriage. But a love like ours encountered hidden sorrows in its precarious future, in its instability, in its lack of indissoluble ties.

"Blanca said to me:

"'I never expected to be loved by a man like you. And after you, I don't see any love or happiness possible for my heart. Joaquín, a love like yours was the need of my life—I was dying without it, and without it I would die tomorrow. Tell me that you'll never forget me.'

"'Let's get married, Blanca!' I responded.

"And Blanca bowed her head in anguish.

"'Yes, let's get married!' I repeated, not understanding that silent despair.

"'How much you love me!' she replied. 'Another man in your place would reject such a notion if I proposed it to him. You, on the contrary—'

"'I, Blanca, am proud of you. I want to show you off to the whole world, I want to be rid of all worry concerning the time to come, I want to know that you're mine forever. Besides, you know my character, you know that I never compromise on matters of honor. Well then, the society in which we live labels our happiness a sin. Why shouldn't we consecrate it at the foot of the altar? I want you pure, I want you noble, I want you saintly. I'll love you then more than now. Accept my hand.'

"'I can't,' that incomprehensible woman answered.

"And this discussion was reproduced a thousand times.

"One day when I held forth against adultery and all immorality, Blanca was deeply touched. She cried, thanked me, and repeated the same things:

"'How much you love me! How good, how great, how noble you are!'

"And all the while the extension of my leave was expiring.

"I had to return to my judgeship, which I explained to Blanca.

"'Separate?' she cried out with infinite anguish.

"'It's your doing,' I said.

"'That's impossible! I worship you, Joaquín.'

"'And I adore you, Blanca.'

"'Give up your career. I'm wealthy. We'll live together!' she exclaimed, covering my mouth so that I couldn't object.

"I kissed her hand and said:

"'I would accept that offer from my wife, making a sacrifice, but from you—'

"'From me!' she said, crying. 'From the mother of your child!'

"'What? You? Blanca!'

"'Yes. God has just told me that I'm a mother. A mother for the first time. You've completed my life, Joaquín, but I no sooner enjoy the pleasure of this absolute bliss than you want to uproot the tree of my joy. You give me a child and you abandon me!'

"'Be my wife, Blanca,' was my only reply. 'Let's bring about the happiness of the angel who's knocking at the doors of life.'

"Blanca was silent for a long time.

"Then she raised her head with an indefinable calm and murmured:

"'I'll be your wife.'

"'Thank you, thank you, darling Blanca!'

"'Listen,' she said a short while later, 'I don't want you to give up your career.'

"'Ah, you sublime woman!'

"'Go back to your court. How long will it take you to arrange your affairs, request more leave from the government and return to Seville?'

"'A month.'

"'A month,' Blanca repeated. 'Fine. I'll wait for you here. Return within a month and I'll be your wife. Today is the 15th of April. By the 15th of May without fail.'

"'Without fail.'

"'Do you swear it?'

"'I swear it.'

"'Once again!' Blanca asked.

"'I swear it.'

"'Do you love me?'

"'With all my heart.'

"'Go, then, and come back to me,' Blanca said.

"She implored me to leave her and set out as soon as possible.

"We said our goodbyes and I set out for ____ that very day."

(3)

"***I*** arrived in ____.

"I made my home ready to receive my wife; I requested and was granted, as you know, another month's leave of absence; and I settled all my affairs with such dispatch that at the end of a fortnight I was free to return to Seville.

"I must tell you that during this time I didn't receive a single letter from Blanca in spite of my having written six to her. I was greatly disturbed by this turn of events. So much so that, although only half of the time period set by my loved one had gone by, I decided to leave for Seville and arrived there on the 30th of April.

"I went immediately to the inn which had been our love nest.

"Blanca had disappeared two days after my departure without informing anyone of her destination.

"Imagine the pain of my disillusionment. Not writing to me that she was leaving. And going off without leaving a forwarding address. Making me lose track of her completely. Slipping away, in short, like a criminal whose crime has been discovered.

"Not even for an instant did it occur to me to remain in Seville until the 15th of May to wait and see if Blanca would return. The intensity of my pain and indignation, and the embarrassment that I felt for having sought the hand of such an adventuress left no room for any hope, any expectation, or any consolation. The reverse would have been an offense to my own moral sense, which was already seeing in Blanca the repugnant, odious being which love or desire had masked until then. Undoubtedly she was a hypocritical, frivolous woman who loved me sensually, but who, anticipating the customary fickleness of her capricious heart, never really thought about our getting married. Pressed, in the end, by my love and my honesty, she had engaged in an awkward pretense in order to escape scot-free. And as for the child announced so joyfully, I had no doubt that it too was another fabrication, another fraud, another cruel joke. It's difficult to understand such perversity in such an intelligent and lovely creature.

"I stayed in Seville for only three days and on May 4th left for Madrid, resigning my position in order to see if my family and the hustle and bustle of the world would make me forget that woman who by turns had been my *heaven* and my *hell.*

"Lastly, about fifteen months ago I had to accept the judgeship of this other town where, as you've seen, I don't live all that happily. And the worst part is that, in the middle of my loathing for Blanca, I detest other women much more—for the simple reason that they aren't her.

"Now are you convinced that I'll never marry?"

VI

Corpus Delicti

Shortly after my friend Zarco finished the account of his love affair, we arrived at the cemetery.

The cemetery of ____ is nothing more than a desolate barren field strewn with wooden crosses and surrounded by an adobe wall. Neither headstones nor graves disturb the monotony of that final abode. Equalized by death, rich and poor and commoner and grandee rest there in the cold earth.

In these unassuming cemeteries, which abound in Spain and which are perhaps the most poetic and the most fitting for its occupants, it frequently happens that in order to bury one body it's necessary to exhume another or, put differently, that every two years another layer of corpses is spread over the earth.

This is due to the small burial grounds and as a consequence around each new grave one sees countless white remains which from time to time are carted off to the common ossuary.

I've seen these ossuaries more than once. And in truth they deserve to be seen. Imagine, in a corner of the cemetery, a kind of pyramid of bones—a hill of multiform ivory, a pile of craniums, femurs, tibias, humeri, broken clavicles, severed spinal columns, rib cages that once enclosed hearts, teeth scattered here and there, phalanges spread about . . . and all of it dried up, cold, dead, barren. Imagine, imagine how ghastly!

And what proximity! Enemies, rivals, spouses, parents and their children—they're all there, and not just together, but scrambled and mixed up bone by bone, like threshed grain, like cut straw. And what a disagreeable sound when one cranium hits another, or when one comes rolling down from the top along those hollow pieces of bygone human beings. And what an insulting laugh the skulls have!

But let's return to our story.

Joaquín and I walked along kicking, sacrilegiously, into numerous inanimate remains, sometimes thinking about the day when other feet would trample ours, sometimes attributing a story to each bone. We were trying to find the secret of life in those craniums where perhaps a genius dwelled or passion raged, and which were now empty like the cell of a deceased monk, or trying to guess—based on shape, hardness, and teeth—if a given skull belonged to a woman, a child, or an old man, when the judge fixed his eyes on one of those ivory globes and stared at it.

"What's this?" he asked, moving back a little. "What's this, my friend? Isn't it a *nail?*"

And as he spoke he used his walking stick to turn over a skull, still quite recent, which retained several thick locks of black hair.

I looked and was as amazed as my friend. The skull was pierced by an iron nail.

The flat head of this nail showed through the crown while the point came out through what had been the roof of the mouth.

What could it mean?

We went from surprise to conjecture to horror.

"I recognize Divine Providence," Zarco finally said. "Here's a dreadful crime that was going to go unpunished and now it reveals itself to the law. I shall fulfill my duty, especially as it appears that God Himself is instructing me to do so by placing the victim's pierced head before my eyes. Yes, sir! I swear that I will not rest until the perpetrator of this horrible crime pays for his atrocity on the scaffold."

VII
Initial Inquiries

My friend Zarco was a model judge.

Fair and a tireless as well as obligatory servant of the administration of justice, he saw in that matter a vast field in which to set in motion all his intelligence, all his zeal, and all his fanaticism (excuse the word) out of compliance with the law.

He had a notary brought in at once and started the proceedings.

After testifying himself to that find, he summoned the gravedigger.

The lugubrious personage was pale and trembling when he appeared before the law. In truth, between those two men any scene had to be horrible. I remember their dialogue verbatim:

JUDGE: Whose skull can this be?

GRAVEDIGGER: Where did Your Honor find it?

JUDGE: In this very spot.

GRAVEDIGGER: Well, then it belongs to a body that, as it was pretty much decomposed, I disinterred yesterday to bury an old woman who died the night before last.

JUDGE: And why did you exhume that body and not one that had been buried longer?

GRAVEDIGGER: I've already told Your Honor: to make space for the old woman. The town council refuses to believe that this cemetery is too small for all the people who are dying now. The result is that the bodies are not allowed to break down in the ground, and I have to take them to the common ossuary before decomposition is total.

JUDGE: And is it possible to learn to whose body this head belongs?

GRAVEDIGGER: Not easily, Your Honor.

JUDGE: Nevertheless, it has to be. So consider it carefully.

GRAVEDIGGER: There may be one way to find out.

JUDGE: Tell me.

GRAVEDIGGER: The dead man's coffin wasn't in bad shape when I hauled it out of the ground, so I took it home to make use of the lid's boards. Maybe they have some sort of mark, like initials or galloons or any other things that are in fashion nowadays to decorate coffins.

JUDGE: Let's see those boards.

While awaiting the gravedigger's return, Zarco ordered a bailiff to wrap the mysterious skull in a piece of cloth and take it home.

When the gravedigger brought the boards we saw, as we were hoping, that on one of them there were a few shreds of a golden galloon which, secured to the wood with metal tacks, would have formed letters and numbers.

But the galloon was torn, and it was impossible to restore the characters.

My friend, however, did not lose heart and had the galloon ripped off completely, and by means of the tacks, or the puncture marks left by others that were missing, he reconstructed the following letters and figures:

A. G. R.
1843
R. I. P.

Zarco beamed with enthusiasm when he made this discovery.

"It's sufficient, more than sufficient," he said joyfully. "Holding on to this thread, I'll go through the labyrinth and unearth everything."*

The bailiff picked up the board, as he had picked up the skull, and we returned to the town.

Without stopping to rest we headed for the nearest parish church.

Zarco asked the priest for the burial register of 1843.

The notary examined it page by page, entry by entry.

The initials A.G.R. did not match any of the deceased.

We went to another parish.

The town has five; at the fourth one that we visited the notary found the following burial entry:

> *At the parish church of Saint ____ in the town of ____ on 4 May 1843 a funeral service and solemn offices for the dead were conducted for DON ALFONSO GUTIÉRREZ DEL ROMERAL, who was buried in the town cemetery. A native and resident of ____, he did not receive the holy sacraments nor did he leave a will, as he died unexpectedly of a cerebral hemorrhage the previous evening at the age of 31. He was married to Doña Gabriela Zahara del Valle, a native of Madrid, and had no children. And let it be known, etc. . . .*

Zarco made a copy of this entry, which was certified by the priest, and we went back to his house.

Along the way the judge said to me:

"I see everything clearly now. These proceedings, which seemed so obscure several hours ago, will be over within a week. What we have here is an 'iron' cerebral hemorrhage, with a head and a point, and it killed Don Alfonso Gutiérrez del Romeral instantly. In other words, we have the nail; now I only need to find the hammer."

VIII

Statements

One neighbor said:

That Don Alfonso Gutiérrez del Romeral, a young and wealthy landowner from that town, had lived a number of years in Madrid and returned in 1840, married to a beautiful lady named Doña Gabriela Zahara;

That the deponent had gone several evenings to socialize with the newlyweds, and he had occasion to observe the peace and happiness enjoyed by the married couple;

That, according to the explanation given by the husband himself, four months prior to the death of Don Alfonso his wife had gone to Madrid to spend some time with her family;

That the young woman returned around the end of April, that is, three and a half months after her departure;

That Don Alfonso's death occurred eight days after her return;

That as the widow fell ill in consequence of the suffering that this loss caused her, she informed her friends that she could not bear to live in a town where everything reminded her of her beloved and lamented husband, and that she left for good in the middle of May, ten or twelve days after her husband's death;

That he could testify to no more, and that it was the truth, according to the oath he had sworn.

Other neighbors gave statements almost identical to the one above.

The late Gutiérrez's servants said, after stating their place of residence:

That the couple did not get along as well as everyone believed;

That the three-and-a-half-month separation which had preceded the last eight days that they lived together as husband and wife was a tacit breakup, the result of profound and puzzling differences between both young people from the beginning of the marriage;

That the night their master died husband and wife had retired to the marital bedroom, as they had been doing since the mistress's return, contrary to their former custom of sleeping apart;

That at midnight they heard the bell ring furiously, along with the mistress's ear-piercing screams;

That they went to help and saw the latter coming out of the bedroom, her hair disheveled, ashen, shaking violently, and screaming in between bitter sobs:

"An attack of apoplexy! Get a doctor! My Alfonso! The master's dying!"

That they entered the bedroom and saw their master lying on the bed, already dead, and that when a doctor came he confirmed that Don Alfonso had died of a cerebral hemorrhage.

The doctor: when queried about the accuracy of the above statement, he said that it was correct in all respects.

The same doctor and two others: having been shown Don Alfonso's skull and asked if death inflicted in that manner could resemble apoplexy in the eyes of a professional, they answered "Yes."

My friend then issued the following writ:

"Whereas the death of Don Alfonso Gutiérrez del Romeral had to have been instantaneous and subsequent to the insertion of the nail in his head;

Whereas, when he died, he was alone with his wife in the connubial bedroom;

Whereas it is impossible to attribute such a death to suicide due to the physical difficulties of execution by one's own hand;

I find Doña Gabriela Zahara del Valle to be the culprit in this case and the perpetrator of the death of her husband, and hereby draw up the appropriate letters rogatory, etc.,etc."

"Tell me, Joaquín," I asked the judge, "do you think Gabriela Zahara will be apprehended?"

"Unquestionably."

"Why are you so certain?"

"Because in the midst of these judicial matters, there is a certain dramatic fatality which never fails. Put more clearly: when bones come out of the grave to testify, there's not much left for the courts to do."

IX

Man Proposes . . .

Despite my friend Zarco's expectations, Gabriela Zahara did not turn up. Letters rogatory, interrogations: everything was futile.

Three months passed.

The case was adjudicated by default.

I left the town of ____, not without promising Zarco that I would return the following year.

X

A Duet in E Major

I spent that winter in Granada.

One night there was a grand ball at the home of the very wealthy Madam ____, who had been kind enough to invite me.

Shortly after arriving at her stately residence, where all the celebrated beauties of Granada's aristocracy had gathered, I noticed one woman who stood out from all the rest, one whose face I would have distinguished from a thousand others, assuming that God would have fashioned another similar to it.

It was my unknown lady, my mysterious and disillusioned lady from the diligence, my traveling companion, seat number 1, about whom I spoke at the beginning of this story.

I hastened to greet her and she recognized me at once.

"Madam," I said to her, "I've kept my promise not to search for you. And I surely did not think it possible to meet you here. Had I known I might not have come, for fear of being an irritant to you. But now that I stand before you, I'm hoping you'll tell me if I may recognize you, if I may talk to you, if the ban that separated us has been lifted."

"I see that you are vindictive," she answered wittily, extending her hand to me. "But I forgive you. How are you?"

"In truth, I don't know," I replied. "My health, the health of my soul—because you wouldn't be asking me about anything else in the middle of a dance—depends on the health of your soul. What I mean is that my happiness can only be a reflection of yours. Has that poor heart healed?"

"Although gallantry may require you to wish it were so," the lady answered, "and although my seeming cheerfulness may make you think so, you know as well as I that wounds of the heart do not heal."

"But, madam, as doctors say, they are treated; they are made bearable; pink skin is spread over the red scar; hope is built upon disappointment."

"But that building is false."

"Like the first one, madam, like every one! 'To want to believe, to want to enjoy,' that's happiness. Mirabeau,* near death, did not accept the generous offer of a young man who wanted to transfuse all his blood into the impoverished arteries of the great man. Don't be like Mirabeau. Drink in a new life from the first virgin heart that offers you its rich blood. And since you do not like gallantries, I'll add in support of my counsel that, speaking in this manner, I am not defending your interests."

"Why do you say that?"

"Because I too am somewhat like Mirabeau—not in my head, but in my blood. I need what you need: a springtime to revitalize me."

"We're most unfortunate! Therefore please do not avoid me in the future."

"Madam, I was going to ask your permission to call on you."

And we said goodbye.

"Who is that woman?" I asked a friend of mine.

"A South American named Mercedes de Méridanueva," he answered me. "That's all I know, and it's much more than what most people know."

XI
FATE

The following day I went to visit my new friend at the Alhambra's Seven Story Inn.

The delightful Mercedes treated me like an intimate friend and invited me to walk with her through that garden of Eden and temple of art, and later to have dinner with her.

We talked about many things during the six hours that we were together, and, as we always came back to the topic of unhappy love affairs, I told her the story of what happened to my friend Zarco.

She listened to it very attentively and, when I finished, started laughing and said to me:

"Felipe, my friend, let this be a lesson to you not to ever fall in love with women you do not know."

"Don't go thinking," I was quick to respond, "that I've made up this story, or that I've told it to you because I imagine that all the mysterious ladies that one encounters on a journey are like the one who deceived my schoolmate."

"Thank you very much, but don't continue," she said, standing up all of a sudden. "Does anyone doubt that at the Seven Story Inn in Granada there may be women lodgers who are not at all like the one who so easily fell in love with your friend at the inn in Seville? As far as I'm concerned, there's no danger of me falling in love with anyone, since I never talk to the same man three times."

"Madam! That's like telling me not to return."

"No, it is simply to inform you that tomorrow at daybreak I'll be leaving Granada, and that we'll probably never see each other again."

"Never? You told me the same thing in Málaga, after our memorable journey, and, nonetheless, we have seen each other again."

"In any case, let's leave it to fate. For my part, I repeat that this is our . . . eternal farewell."

After saying these solemn words, Mercedes extended her hand to me and made a deep bow.

I went away profoundly moved, not only by the cold and disdainful expressions with which that woman had again dismissed me from her life (as when we separated in Málaga), but also by the hopeless sorrow that I saw show on her face while she was trying to smile and say goodbye to me for the last time.

For the last time! Oh! I wish it had been the last time!

XII
FORTUNE'S PRANKS

Several days later my affairs once again took me to see Joaquín Zarco.

My friend, still depressed and lonely, cheered up considerably when I arrived.

He had not been able to learn a thing about Blanca, nor had he been able to forget about her, not even for a single moment.

Undoubtedly that woman was his destiny—his *heaven* or his *hell,* as the poor devil was wont to say.

We shall soon see that he was not mistaken in this superstitious belief.

The evening of the very day of my arrival we were in his office reading the latest proceedings instituted to effect the capture of Gabriela Zahara del Valle, all of them futile to be sure, when a bailiff entered and handed the judge a note that read: "At the *Lion Inn* there is a lady who wishes to speak to Judge Zarco."

"Who brought this?" Joaquín asked.

"A servant."

"Sent by whom?"

"He didn't say."

"And this servant—"

"Left immediately."

Joaquín reflected and then said gloomily:

"A lady? To speak to me? I don't know why, but such a meeting alarms me. What do you think, Felipe?"

"That it's your duty as a judge to go. It may have to do with Gabriela Zahara."

"You're right. I'll go," Zarco said, running his hand over his forehead.

And, taking two pistols and wrapping himself in his cape, he left without letting me accompany him.

Two hours later he returned.

He was agitated, tremulous, and stammering.

I quickly understood that an intense joy was the cause of his excitement.

Zarco embraced me convulsively, exclaiming in a loud, ecstatic, choked voice:

"Ah, my friend, if you knew! If only you knew!"

"I know nothing," I said. "What happened?"

"I'm happy now. I'm the happiest man in the world."

"What's going on?

"The note asking me to go to the inn—"

"Yes?"

"It was from her!"

"From whom? From Gabriela Zahara?"

"No, no, not at all! Who's thinking about misfortune now? It was from her! From the other one!'

"But who's the other one?"

"Who else? Blanca—my love, my life, the mother of my child!"

"Blanca?" I asked in astonishment. "But didn't you tell me she had deceived you?"

"Ah, no! That was delusion on my part."

"The one you're suffering now?"

"No. The one I suffered then."

"Explain yourself."

"Listen: Blanca adores me."

"Go on. Your saying so proves nothing."

"When Blanca and I separated on the 15th of April, we agreed to meet in Seville on the 15th of May. Shortly after my departure she received a letter saying that she needed to be in Madrid to deal with family matters, and, having a month until my return, she left for the capital and then went back to Seville sooner than the 15th of May. Now: more impatient than Blanca, I showed up for our meeting two weeks ahead of time, and, not finding her at the inn, I thought she had deceived me and I didn't wait. In short, I've endured two years of torment because of my own rash behavior."

"But a letter would have prevented all of it."

"She says she had forgotten the name of that town, where, you'll recall, I immediately resigned as public prosecutor in order to go to Madrid."

"Ah, my poor friend!" I exclaimed. "I see that you're trying to convince yourself, trying to console yourself. So much the better.

So let's see: when are you getting married? Because I assume that once the fog of jealousy has been dispelled, the sun of matrimony will shine brilliantly."

"Don't laugh!" Zarco exclaimed. "You'll be my best man."

"Gladly. Oh, the child! What about your child?"

"It died."

"That too! Well, sir," I said, bewildered. "May God perform a miracle."

"What?"

"I mean—may He make you happy."

XIII
God Disposes

We were at this point in our conversation when we heard loud knocks on the outside door.

It was two o'clock in the morning.

Joaquín and I shuddered without knowing why.

An assistant opened the door and a few moments later a man entered the office. He was nearly out of breath, but elated, and exclaimed between gasps:

"Good news, Judge, very good news! We've done it!"

It was the public prosecutor.

"Explain yourself, my friend," Zarco said, holding out a chair for him. "What's happened that you come at such a late hour and in such good spirits?"

"What's happened? Nothing of much importance! What's happened is that Gabriela Zahara—"

"What? How?" Zarco and I interrupted at the same time.

"—has just been apprehended!"

"Apprehended!" shouted the judge, overjoyed.

"Yes, sir, apprehended," the prosecutor repeated. "The Civil Guard has been following her for a month, and the night watchman who usually accompanies me from the casino to my home has just informed me that we have her in safekeeping in the jail of this very noble town."

"Then, let's go to the jail," the judge said to him. "We'll take her statement now, tonight. Please notify the court clerk. Due to the gravity of this case I also want you present at the interrogation.

And have someone send for the gravedigger so that he himself can display Don Alfonso Gutiérrez's head, which at the moment is in the possession of the bailiff. I've given consideration for some time to this awful confrontation between husband and wife, certain that the latter won't be able to deny her crime when she sees that iron nail which, in the skull's mouth, looks like an accusing tongue.

"As for you," Zarco then turned to me, "you'll serve as secretary so you can witness, without breaking the law, scenes of great interest."

I didn't say anything to him. My unfortunate friend was given over to his judicial joy—if you'll pardon the expression—and had not conceived the horrible suspicion which, doubtless, has already occurred to all of you, a suspicion which of course bored into me and pierced my heart with its iron claws. Gabriela and Blanca, both of whom had arrived in that town the same night, might be one and the same person!

"Tell me," I asked the public prosecutor while Zarco was preparing to leave, "where was Gabriela when the police arrested her?"

"At the *Lion Inn,*" he replied.

My anguish knew no bounds.

Nevertheless, I couldn't do anything or say anything without compromising Zarco, nor should I have poisoned my friend's soul by telling him my terrible misgivings, which the facts might refute. Besides, assuming that Gabriela and Blanca *were* one and the same person, how would it help the poor devil for me to point that out to him beforehand? What could he do in such a dreadful quandary? Flee? It was incumbent upon me to prevent such incriminating behavior. Turn the case over to someone else, feigning a sudden indisposition? That would be tantamount to abandoning Blanca in whose defense he could do so much—if the case seemed defensible to him. My duty, therefore, was to keep silent and let God's justice be done.

At any rate, such were my thoughts during that unexpected turn of events, when there was neither time nor opportunity for immediate solutions. The catastrophe was unfolding with tragic haste. The prosecutor had already transmitted Zarco's orders to the bailiffs, one of whom had gone to the jail for the purpose of preparing the courtroom to receive the judge. The commander of the Civil Guard appeared at that moment to report in person—so pleased was he with the outcome—on Gabriela Zahara's imprisonment. And a number of night owls, members of the casino and the judge's friends, having heard the news, were also heading toward the jail to nose about and get a preview of the emotions of the terrible day when such a beautiful and prominent lady would mount the scaffold. In short, there was nothing left to do but go to the edge of the abyss, praying to God that Gabriela not be Blanca.

So I concealed my uneasiness and kept my fears to myself, and about four o'clock in the morning I followed the judge, the public prosecutor, the court clerk, the commander of the Civil Guard, and a crowd of bystanders and bailiffs who moved merrily to the jailhouse.

XIV
THE TRIBUNAL

The gravedigger had already arrived.

The courtroom was brightly lighted.

On the table stood a black wooden box which contained Don Alfonso Gutiérrez del Romeral's skull.

The judge took his seat; the public prosecutor sat on his right; and the commander of the Civil Guard, as a courtesy that went beyond forensic procedures, was also invited to witness the interrogation, given the interest that those sensational proceedings had awakened in him, as in the whole town. The clerk and I sat down on the judge's left, while the jailer and bailiffs gathered at the door where there were a number of spectators whose financial standing had gained them entry to the feared jailhouse to witness such a solemnity, but who would have to be content with just seeing the accused so as not to violate the secrecy of the hearing.

With the court of justice constituted in this manner, the judge rang the bell and said to the jailer:

"Have Doña Gabriela Zahara brought in."

I felt as if I were dying, and, instead of watching the door, I was watching Zarco to read in his face the solution of the problem that had me so concerned.

I soon saw my friend turn deathly pale, raise his hand to his throat as if to stifle a howl of pain, and look at me for help.

"Don't say anything!" I cautioned him, putting my forefinger on my lips.

And then I added, in a perfectly ordinary voice, as if responding to an observation of his:

"I knew it."

The poor devil tried to stand up.

"Your Honor!" I said at once with such force of expression that he understood the full magnitude of his duties and the risks he was running.

He froze, horribly, like someone who is trying to carry an enormous weight and, in the end mastering his shock, his face became as rigid as stone. Had it not been for the fire in his eyes, one might have thought that that man was dead.

And the *man* was dead; only the *judge* lived in him now. When I had convinced myself of that, I looked, like everyone else, at the accused.

Imagine my surprise and consternation, which were almost the same as the miserable Zarco's. Gabriela Zahara was not only my friend's Blanca, his lover from Seville, the woman with whom he had just been reconciled at the *Lion Inn,* but also my unknown lady from Málaga, my friend from Granada—the ever beautiful South American, Mercedes de Méridanueva.

All those fantastic women combined into one, an indisputable one, a real and tangible one, one upon whom weighed the accusation of having murdered her husband, one who was condemned to death by default.

Now then: this accused woman, this sentenced woman, could she be innocent? Would she be able to tell the truth? Would she be acquitted?

This was my sole and supreme hope, and it should also have been that of my poor friend Zarco.

XV
The Trial

THE JUDGE IS A LAW WHO SPEAKS
AND THE LAW A MUTE JUDGE.
THE LAW SHOULD BE LIKE DEATH,
WHICH FORGIVES NO ONE.

—MONTESQUIEU

Gabriela—let's call her, at last, by her real name—was exceedingly pale, but also very tranquil. Was that calm a sign of her innocence or did it confirm the insensitivity typical of hardened criminals? Was Don Alfonso's widow trusting in the righteousness of her position or in the weakness of her judge?

My doubts were soon resolved.

Until then the accused had looked only at Zarco—I don't know whether to infuse courage into him and show him how to conceal emotion, whether to threaten him with dangerous tales, or whether to give him silent testimony that his Blanca could not have committed murder. But, undoubtedly observing the judge's frightful impassivity, she must have been afraid, and she glanced at the other people present as if seeking in their sympathy moral support for her good or bad cause.

Then she saw me, and a sudden blush, which seemed propitious, tinged her face scarlet.

But she recovered at once and reverted to her paleness and calm.

Zarco finally emerged from the stupor which had numbed him, and, in a harsh and hard voice like the rod of justice, asked his former lover and fiancée:

"What is your name?"

"Gabriela Zahara del Valle de Gutiérrez del Romeral," answered the accused in a soft, quiet voice.

Zarco trembled slightly. He had just heard that his Blanca had never existed. She herself told him—she, who just three hours before had agreed to the marriage proposal of old!

Fortunately no one was looking at the judge; they all had their eyes fixed on Gabriela, whose singular beauty and soft, gentle voice were regarded as signs of inculpability. Even the simple black dress that she wore seemed to speak in her defense.

Once he recovered from his confusion, Zarco said to the gravedigger in a formidable voice, like a gambler who wagers his entire stake on one hand:

"Perform your duty and open that coffin." And he pointed at the black box containing Don Alfonso's skull.

"You, madam," the judge continued, looking at the accused with fire in his eyes, "approach and say if you recognize that head."

The gravedigger took the lid off and showed the open box to the widow in mourning.

Gabriela, who had come forward, stared at the inside of the so-called "coffin," and the first thing she saw was the nailhead, which protruded from the top of the skull.

A sharp, piercing, mortal scream, like the kind that is triggered by sudden fear or that foreshadows madness, escaped from Gabriela's lips, and she flinched, tearing her hair and stammering in a low voice:

"Alfonso! Alfonso!"

And she appeared stupid from shock.

"She's the one!" we all murmured, turning toward Joaquín.

"So you recognize the nail that killed your husband?" the judge asked her, rising with a terrible expression, as if he himself were coming out of the grave.

"Yes, Your Honor," Gabriela replied mechanically, with an intonation and movement characteristic of idiocy.

"In other words, you admit you murdered him?" the judge continued with such anguish that the accused came around and shuddered violently.

"Your Honor," she then said, "I have no wish to live any longer, but before I die I want to tell my story."

Zarco fell back in his chair, stunned, and looked at me as if to ask: Now what is she going to say?

I too was stunned.

Gabriela heaved a deep sigh and spoke as follows:

"I am going to confess, and my defense will consist of my very confession, although it won't suffice to save me from the scaffold. Please listen, all of you.

"Why deny the obvious? I was alone with my husband when he died. The servants and the doctor must have testifed to that. Therefore, only I could have killed him in the manner revealed by his skull, which has risen from the grave in his behalf. So I do plead guilty to this gruesome crime, but it behooves you to know that a man forced me to commit it."

Zarco trembled upon hearing these words. However, he mastered his fear as he had mastered his pity and exclaimed courageously:

"His name, madam! Tell me at once the wretched creature's name!"

Gabriela stared at the judge with boundless worship, like a mother at her suffering child, and added in a melancholy voice:

"I could, with a single word, drag him down to the abyss into which he caused me to fall. I could drag him to the scaffold so that he wouldn't remain in this world and perhaps curse me upon marrying another woman. But I refuse to do that. I will not reveal his name because he loved me and I love him. And I love him although I know he will do nothing to prevent my death."

The judge extended his right hand as if he were going to reach out to her, but she admonished him with an affectionate glance which in effect said: Don't give yourself away!

Zarco lowered his head.

Gabriela continued.

"I was forced to marry a man I abhorred, a man that I grew to abhor even more as my husband because of his meanness and shameful behavior. I spent three years in torment—resigned, and trapped in a loveless, miserable marriage. One day, reflecting on the purgatory of my life and searching, as an innocent woman, for a way out, I saw through the iron bars that imprisoned me one of those angels that pass by and release souls deserving of heaven. I clutched on to his tunic, saying to him: 'Give me happiness.' And the angel said to me: 'You can no longer be happy.' 'Why?' 'Because you aren't now.' In other words, the odious man who until then had tormented me was preventing me from flying away with that angel to the heaven of love and happiness. Can you imagine anything more absurd than reasoning such as this concerning my fate?

"I'll put it more clearly: I had met a man who was worthy of me, and I was worthy of him. We loved each other, we adored each other, but he didn't know of the existence of my in-name-only husband. And of course he wanted to marry me, and as he wouldn't countenance anything illegal or unseemly he threatened to leave me if we didn't get married. He was an exceptional man, a model of integrity, a person of severe and noble manner whose only failing in life consisted of having loved me to an extreme. It's true that we were going to have an illegitimate child, but it's also true that the accomplice in my dishonor never stopped imploring me to wed. I'm certain that if I had said to him, 'I've deceived you—I'm not a widow and my husband's alive,' he would have left me, and detested me, and cursed me. So I invented a thousand excuses, a thousand arguments, and he responded to all of them with: 'Be my wife.' I *couldn't* be his wife, and he believed that I didn't *want* to be and began to detest me. What was I to do? I resisted, I cried, I begged, but he, even after learning that we had a child, repeated that he wouldn't see me again until I agreed to marry him. But I was already married and bound to a contemptible man, and between killing him or causing the misfortune of my child, that of the man I adored, and my own, I opted for snuffing out the useless, miserable life of the one who was our scourge. And so . . . I killed my husband, believing that I was discharging an act of justice on a criminal who had deceived me horribly when he married me, but then God punished me, because my lover abandoned me. After a time we met again. But why, dear God? Oh, let me die soon! Yes, let me die soon!"

Gabriela fell silent for a moment, overcome by tears.

Zarco had covered his face with his hands, as if he were meditating, but I could see that he was shaking like a leaf.

"Your Honor," Gabriela repeated with renewed energy, "let me die soon!'

Zarco made a sign to have the accused taken away.

Gabriela left with a firm step, not without first giving me a frightful look, in which there was more pride than remorse.

XVI
THE SENTENCE

I shall refrain from relating the formidable struggle that broke out in Zarco's soul, one which lasted until the day the judgment was upheld. I'm incapable of making you understand those fierce battles. I'll only say that the judge vanquished the man, and Joaquín Zarco sentenced Gabriela Zahara to death.

The following day the transcript of the trial was dispatched to the superior court in Seville for review, and at the same time Zarco said farewell to me with these words:

"Wait for me here until I return. Look out for the poor thing, but don't visit her because your presence would humiliate her instead of consoling her. Don't ask me where I'm going and don't be afraid that I'll commit the hideous crime of suicide. Goodbye, and forgive the grief I've caused you."

Three weeks later the superior court upheld the death sentence.

Gabriela Zahara was sent to the jail's chapel to await execution.

XVII
THE FINAL JOURNEY

The day of the execution arrived and Zarco had not returned, nor was there any news from him.

A huge throng waited at the door of the jail to see the condemned woman come out.

I was part of the crowd, because although I had respected my friend's wishes by not visiting Gabriela in her prison, I thought it my duty to represent Zarco at that supreme moment and accompany his one-time lover to the foot of the scaffold.

When Gabriela appeared, I scarcely recognized her. She had become horribly emaciated and barely had the strength to raise to her lips the crucifix that she kissed time and again.

"Here I am, madam. Can I help you in any way?" I asked when she passed by me.

She stared at me, hollow-eyed, and when she recognized me, exclaimed:

"Oh, thank you, thank you! What great solace you are giving me in my final hour. Father," she said, turning to her confessor, "may I speak a few words to this generous friend while we walk?"

"Yes, my daughter," the priest answered, "but keep your mind on God."

Gabriela then asked me:

"And Joaquín?"

"He's not here."

"May God make him happy. When you see him, tell him to forgive me so that God will. Tell him that I still love him, even though my love for him is the cause of my death."

"I want to see you resigned."

"I am! How much I wish to be in the presence of my eternal Father! How many centuries I intend to spend weeping at His feet, until I can get Him to recognize me as His daughter and forgive me my many sins!"

We arrived at the foot of the fatal ladder, where we had to separate.

Tears, perhaps the last ones that remained in her heart, welled up in Gabriela's eyes as she stammered:

"Tell him that I went to my death blessing him."

At that moment a clamor arose among the crowd, which began to shout in unison:

"A pardon! A pardon!"

And along the wide passage opened up by the throng a man was seen rapidly approaching on horseback, a piece of paper in one hand and a white handkerchief in the other.

It was Zarco.

"A pardon! A pardon!" he too was shouting.

He finally dismounted and, accompanied by the chief official, headed for the gallows.

Gabriela, who had already climbed several rungs, stopped, looked lovingly at her lover, and murmured:

"God bless you!"

And she promptly lost consciousness.

As soon as the remission was read and the proceeding formalized, the priest and Joaquín rushed to untie the pardoned woman's hands.

But no mercy could help her now. Gabriela Zahara was dead.

XVIII
Moral

Today Zarco is one of the best judges in Havana. He has married and can be considered happy, because sorrow is not misfortune when harm has not been done deliberately to anyone.

The son that his loving wife has just given to him will dispel the vague aura of melancholy that occasionally clouds my friend's brow.

CÁDIZ, 1853

La corneta de llaves

The Cornet

Where there's a will there's a way.

I

"**Don** Basilio, play the cornet and we'll dance! It's not hot under these trees."

"Yes, yes, Don Basilio, play the cornet!"

"Bring Don Basilio the cornet that Joaquín is learning to play on."

"It's not a very good one. Will you play it, Don Basilio?"

"No."

"What do you mean,'no'?"

"I mean no."

"Why won't you?"

"Because I don't know how."

"Don't know how? Are you trying to hoodwink us?"

"No doubt he wants us to butter him up."

"Come on. We all know that you were the infantry bandmaster."

"And that nobody played the cornet better than you."

"And that you played at the royal palace, in Espartero's day." *

"And that you have a pension."

"Come on, Don Basilio, take pity on us."

"All right, it's true. I did play the cornet. I was a . . . an artist as you say now, but it's also true that twelve years ago I gave away my cornet to a poor discharged musician and that since then I haven't so much as hummed a tune."

"What a shame!"

"Another Rossini!"

"Oh, but you have to play for us this afternoon!"

"Out here in the country everything is permissible."
"And remember that it's my saint's day, Grandpapa!"
"Hurray! Hurray! The cornet's here!"
"Yes, let him play!
"A waltz."
"No, a polka."
"A polka? Positively not. A fandango!"
"Yes, yes! A fandango! The national dance!"
"I'm very sorry, my children, but it's not possible for me to play."
"But you're so kind!"
"And so obliging!"
"And your little grandson is begging you!"
"And your niece."
"Leave me alone, for heaven's sake! I've said I won't play."
"Why not?"
"Because I don't remember how, and because, in addition, I swore that I wouldn't learn again."
"To whom did you swear it?"
"To myself, to a dead man, and to your poor mother, my child."
All their faces suddenly fell as he spoke these words.
"Oh, if you knew at what cost I learned to play the cornet!" added the old man.
"The story! The story!" exclaimed the young people. "Tell us the story!"
"Well," said Don Basilio, "it is quite a story. All right. Listen to it and you'll judge whether or not I can play the cornet."
And sitting under a tree, surrounded by curious and genial young people, he told the story of his music lessons.
So too did Mazzepa, Byron's hero,* relate one night to Charles XII, under another tree, the terrible story of his horseback riding lessons.
Let's listen to Don Basilio.

II

"***Seventeen*** years ago civil war was raging in Spain.
"Carlos and Isabel were fighting for the crown,* and the Spanish people, divided into two sides, were shedding blood in a fratricidal struggle.
"I had a friend named Ramón Gómez, a lieutenant of chasseurs

in my battalion, the best man I've ever known. We grew up together, left high school together, fought a thousand times together, and wanted to die for freedom together. Oh, I'm tempted to say that he was more liberal than I or anyone else in the entire army.

"But then our commanding officer did Ramón an injustice—one of those abuses of authority that discredit the most honorable career, an arbitrary act, in short, which caused the lieutenant of chasseurs to desert the ranks of his brothers, and caused the friend to leave his friends, the liberal to go over to the conservatives, and the subordinate officer to kill his lieutenant colonel. Ramón was much too proud to tolerate insults or injustices from a living soul.

"Neither my threats nor my entreaties were sufficient to dissuade him from his purpose. He had made up his mind. He would exchange Isabel's helmet for Carlos's white beret, even though he mortally hated the latter's rebel followers.

"At the time we were in the principality of Navarre,* about ten miles away from the enemy.

"It was the night that Ramón intended to desert, a cold, rainy night, and dreary and gloomy, the eve of a battle.

"Around midnight Ramón came into my quarters.

"I was asleep.

"'Basilio,' he whispered in my ear.

"'Who is it?'

"'It's me. Come to say goodbye.'

"'So you're going now?'

"'Yes. Goodbye.'

"And he grasped one of my hands.

"'Listen,' he continued, 'if there's a battle tomorrow, as everyone thinks, and we meet in it. . . .'

"'I know: we're friends.'

"'Right. We'll embrace and then we'll fight. I expect to die tomorrow because I'll ride roughshod over everything until I kill the lieutenant colonel. As for you, Basilio, don't put yourself at risk. Glory is fleeting.'

"'And life?'

"'You're right. Become a commandant. The pay isn't fleeting, at least not until one has spent it. Oh, all that has ended for me!'

"'What gloomy thoughts!' I said, deeply affected. 'Tomorrow we'll both survive the battle.'

"'Then let's decide on a time and place to meet afterward.'

"'Where?'

"'At the San Nicolás Hermitage, at one in the morning. If one of us doesn't come it'll be because he's dead. Are we agreed?'

"'Agreed.'

"'Then . . . goodbye!'

"'Goodbye!'

"We embraced warmly after speaking these words and Ramón disappeared in the darkness of the night."

III

"***As*** we expected the Carlist rebels attacked us the following day.

"The action was very bloody and lasted from three in the afternoon until nightfall.

"About five o'clock my battalion was furiously assaulted by a force from Alava* commanded by Ramón.

"Ramón now wore the insignia of a commandant and the white beret of the Carlists!

"I gave the order to fire on Ramón and he gave the order to fire on me, and his men and mine began to fight in hand-to-hand combat.

"We were victorious and Ramón had to retreat with the greatly reduced ranks of his Alavese troops, but not before he himself had killed, with a pistol shot, the man who just the day before had been his lieutenant colonel, a man who attempted in vain to defend himself from Ramón's fury.

"At six the tide turned against our army and part of my poor company and I were cut off and forced to surrender.

"So I was taken prisoner to the small town of ____, occupied by the Carlists since the start of that campaign and where, presumably, I would be shot immediately.

"At that time it was a war without quarter."

IV

"***It*** struck one o'clock on the night of that fateful day, the hour of my meeting with Ramón.

"I was locked up in one of the cells of the town jail.

"I asked about my friend.

"'He's a brave man!' I was told. 'He killed a lieutenant colonel, but he must have died in the final moments of action.'

"'What? Why do you say that?'

"'Because he hasn't returned from the battlefield nor have the men under his command today been able to give an account of him.'

"Oh, how much I suffered that night!

"I had one hope: that Ramón was waiting for me at San Nicolás Hermitage, which would explain why he hadn't returned to the rebel camp.

"'How sad he'll be when I don't show up for the meeting,' I thought. 'He'll think I'm dead. And am I not, in reality, close to my last hour? The rebels always shoot their prisoners now, just as we do.'

"And so dawn broke the next morning.

"A chaplain entered my cell.

"All my comrades were asleep.

"'Time to die!' I exclaimed upon seeing the priest.

"'Yes,' he replied gently.

"'Now?'

"'No. In three hours.'

"Shortly afterward my comrades awoke, and endless screams, sobs, and curses filled the confines of the jail."

V

"***Every*** man who is going to die usually latches on to an idea of some sort and doesn't let go of it.

"Whether it was a nightmare, a fever, or madness, that's what happened to me. The idea of Ramón—Ramón alive, Ramón dead, Ramón in heaven, Ramón at the hermitage—took possession of my mind in such a way that I thought of nothing else during those hours of agony.

"They removed my captain's uniform and gave me a busby and an enlisted man's old cloak.

"And dressed like that I was marched to be executed with my nineteen comrades in misfortune.

"Only one had been pardoned—because he happened to be a musician. Carlists at that time were sparing the lives of musicians because there was a great shortage of them in their army."

"And were you a musician, Don Basilio? Is that what saved your life?" asked all the young people at once.

"No, my children," replied the veteran. "I was not a musician!

"Ranks were closed with us in the middle.

"I was number eleven; in other words, I was the eleventh one slated to die.

"Then I thought about my wife and daughter—about you and your mother, my child!

"The firing began.

"Those shots were driving me mad!

"As I was blindfolded, I didn't see my comrades fall.

"I tried to count the volleys in order to know, a moment before dying, that my stay in this world was coming to an end.

"But I lost the count before the third discharge.

"Oh, those shots will boom forever and a day in my heart and in my brain, as they did that day!

"First I thought I heard them a thousand miles away, then I thought I heard them go off inside my head.

"And there was no end to them!

"'Now!' I thought.

"And the shot would ring out and I was still alive.

"'This time!' I finally said to myself.

"And I realized that I was being grabbed by the shoulders and shaken . . . and that there was shouting.

"I fell down.

"I stopped thinking.

"But I was overcome by something like a deep sleep.

"And I dreamed that I had been executed by a firing squad."

VI

"Afterward I dreamed that I was lying on a cot, in my prison.

"I couldn't see.

"I raised my hand to my eyes as if to remove a bandage and discovered that they were open, wide open. Had I been blinded?

"No. It was because the prison was in total darkness.

"I heard a bell tolling . . . and I shuddered.

"It was the bell to pray for the souls in purgatory.

"'It's nine o'clock,' I thought. 'But of what day?'

"A shadow, darker than the dismal prison air, bent over me.

"It resembled a man.

"And the others? The other eighteen?

"They had all been executed by a firing squad.

"And I?

"I was alive or delirious inside a tomb.

"My lips automatically muttered a name—the same name as always, my nightmare:

"'Ramón!'

"'What do you want?' answered the shadow at my side.

"I trembled.

"'My God!' I exclaimed. 'Am I in the other world?'

"'No!' said the same voice.

"'Ramón, are you alive?'

"'Yes.'

"'And I?'

"'You are too.'

"'Where am I? Is this San Nicolás Hermitage? Am I not a prisoner? Have I dreamed all this?'

"'No, Basilio, you haven't dreamed anything. Listen.'"

VII

"'**As** you probably know, yesterday I killed the lieutenant colonel in a fair fight. I am avenged! Later, mad with rage, I kept on killing and killing, until after nightfall, until there wasn't a living soul on the battlefield.

"'When the moon came out, I remembered our meeting and headed for San Nicolás Hermitage with the idea of waiting for you.

"'It must have been ten o'clock. We were to meet at one and the night before I hadn't slept a wink, so I fell fast asleep.

"'At the stroke of one I awoke with a start and cried out.

"'I was dreaming that you had died.

"'I glanced around and saw that I was alone.

"'What had become of you?

"'It struck two . . . three . . . four o'clock. What a night of anguish!

"'You weren't coming.

"'Undoubtedly you were dead.

"'The day broke.

"'I then left the hermitage and came to this town in search of the Carlists.

"'I arrived at sunup.

"'Everybody believed that I had died the evening before.

"'So when they saw me they embraced me and the general heaped praises on me.

"'I learned immediately that twenty-one prisoners were going to be shot.

"'A premonition stirred my soul.

"'Can Basilio be one of them?' I wondered.

"'And I ran to the place of execution.

"'The lineup was formed.

"'I heard a few shots.

"'They had begun the executions.

"'I looked around . . . and couldn't see.

"'I was blinded by grief, faint from fear.

"'But I finally recognized you.

"'You were going to be shot!

"'There were only two victims left before you.

"'What could I do?

"'I went crazy; I screamed; I put my arms around your shoulders and, in a hoarse, heartrending, fierce voice, I exclaimed:

"'Not this one! Not this one, General!

"'The general who commanded the firing squad, and who knew me so well on account of my actions the day before, asked me:

"'Why? Is he a musician?'

"'That word for me was what it would be for an old man blind from birth to suddenly see the sun in all its brilliance.

"'The light of hope shone so unexpectedly in my eyes that it blinded them.

"'A musician!' I exclaimed. 'Yes, yes, General! He's a musician! A great musician!

"'In the meantime you lay unconscious.

"'What instrument does he play?' asked the general.

"'The, ah, the . . . the . . . I've got it! The cornet!'

"'Is a cornet player needed?' asked the general, turning to the band.

"'Five seconds, five centuries, the answer took.

"'Yes, General, one is needed,' replied the bandmaster.

"'All right. Remove that man from the ranks and let the execution continue at once,' the Carlist general ordered.

"'I then took you in my arms and brought you to this prison cell.'"

VIII

"***As*** soon as Ramón stopped talking, I stood up and said to him—how, I don't know, what with laughing and crying and shaking—as I embraced him:

"'I owe you my life!'

"'We'll see!' Ramón answered.

"'What do you mean?' I asked.

"'Do you know how to play the cornet?'

"'No.'

"'Then you don't owe me your life, and I've endangered mine without saving yours.'

"My heart froze.

"'And music?' asked Ramón. 'Do you know any music?'

"'Very little. You remember what they taught us in school.'

"'Very little indeed. Next to nothing. You'll die for sure. And so will I—for being a traitor and a liar. Just imagine. The band you're to play with will be organized in fifteen days.'

"'Fifteen days!'

"'Exactly. And as you won't be playing the cornet—because God isn't going to perform a miracle—the two of us will be shot for sure.'

"'You shot!' I exclaimed. 'You! Because of me! Me! The one who owes you his life! Oh, no! Heaven will not allow it! In fifteen days I'll learn music and how to play the cornet.'

"Ramón started laughing."

IX

"***What*** else do you want me to tell you, my children?

"In fifteen days—such is the power of the will—in fifteen days and the corresponding fifteen nights, because I didn't sleep or rest a moment for half a month, in fifteen days, astonishingly, I learned to play the cornet!

"What days they were!

"Ramón and I would go out in the country and spend hour after hour with a certain musician who every day came from a nearby village to give me lessons.

"*Escape!* I see the word on your lips. Nothing was more impossible. I was a prisoner, closely watched, and Ramón didn't want to escape without me.

"And I didn't talk or think or eat.

"I was mad, and my obsession was music and the cornet, the diabolical cornet.

"I wanted to learn and I did learn!

"And had I been dumb, I would've talked.

"And had I been paralytic, I would've walked.

"And had I been blind, I would've seen.

"Because I *wanted to!*

"Oh, the will makes up for everything! WHERE THERE'S A WILL THERE'S A WAY.

"I *wanted to:* that was the key.

"I *wanted to:* and I succeeded. Children, learn the meaning of *wanting to* do something.

"So I saved my life.

"But I went mad.

"And while mad, my madness was artistry.

"For three years, the cornet never left my hands.

"*Do-re-mi-fa-sol-la-ti-do:* this was my life during that time.

"All I did was play.

"Ramón did not leave my side.

"I emigrated to France, and in France I continued playing the cornet.

"I *was* the cornet. I sang when my lips were on the mouthpiece of the cornet.

"People, towns, stars of the art world—they all gathered to hear me.

"The whole thing was a wonder, a marvel.

"The cornet submitted to my fingers; it became flexible; it moaned, cried, shouted, and roared; it imitated a bird, a beast, and a human sob. My lungs were made of iron.

"Thus did I live for two years.

"At the end of that time my friend died.

"Looking at his body, I came to my senses.

"And when, in my right mind, I picked up the cornet one day, I found to my astonishment that I didn't know how to play it.

"Now: will you still ask me to make music for you to dance?"

MADRID, 1854

El asistente

The Orderly

How sweet are the hours that follow a meal with animated friends, when sherry flows, when cigar smoke envelops the diners, imagination borne upward in the wake of its voluptuous swirls; when the finger of memory wistfully leafs through the book of the past, and secrets spill from every heart, and masks fall from every face, and anecdotes, jokes, stories, tales, dramas, and poems pour out.

Everyone tells something—even the most taciturn and circumspect of the group bares his soul. The servants or waiters (depending on whether it is a home or a restaurant) have left the dining room. The conversation is no longer about music, politics, literature, or religion; the conversation is about life, time, hope, and the world as we know it. Every spirit has risen to the same height, and from that philosophical summit casts backward glances at the plains of existence and calm glances at days on the wane.

Byron has said: "I enjoy a fire, the crackling of burning logs, a bottle of champagne, and a good conversation."

We had all of that, except the burning logs, because it was the beginning of May and we were in Andalusia, in Granada, in the Alhambra, at the Seven Story Inn.

We had spoken of many people—of Byron himself, the Duke of Reichstadt, Louis XVII, Pope Joan, Prester John of the Indies, Sebastian of Portugal,* and illustrious dead, when, by what means I don't know, we ended up talking about dogs, monkeys, Hottentots, and, lastly, orderlies.

A very young, very brave, and very learned captain, to whom I dedicate this account, then addressed the group and told us, in pretty much these words, the following story:

"I want you to have an exact idea of this noble type, the orderly, whose nature you have formed in part. Then you may draw whatever conclusions you wish for or against Christian civilization and civilization in general; you may continue to discuss Manicheanism, animals' instincts, the good and bad of human behavior, and the social form best suited to our fallen nature. As for me, a practical man, I'll content myself with relating an episode to you, or rather, confessing a fault."

"A story!" we all exclaimed, settling ourselves comfortably in our chairs. "This is how all good conversation draws to a close! Let the captain speak!"

The latter lighted his third cigar and began in a sad, dignified manner:

"From the time I left school and signed up for the army until now, a stretch of ten years, I've had only two orderlies—the one you've just seen and one named García, who is the protagonist of this story."

The captain's voice quavered as he spoke the name.

He took a sip of coffee and continued.

"García was a reenlisted soldier, twenty-eight or thereabout, and a native of Totana.* He looked like an Arab, or rather, a Tunisian, with black eyes and dark skin; he was a man of few words, unquestioned courage, and very intense likes and dislikes.

"I must point out to you, however, that the only likes and dislikes that I ever saw in him were reflections of my own. He loved whomever I loved and detested whomever I detested.

"I never knew him to have a girl or any kind of vice, nor did I know when he ate and slept. I can only say that at all times he was within earshot, ready to satisfy my slightest whim, whether or not we had money, whether it was night or day, whether the land baked under a summer sun or was covered by three feet of snow.

"That man constituted my entire family when I was away from home, which was almost always, so I should've loved him a great deal, and perhaps I did. Oh, yes! I realized it afterward. I did indeed love him, but it never occurred to me to be aware of it. This is very common in men of my character. I'm the same way now with my wife. Intractable and diabolic. In any case, let's get back to the subject.

"From what I'm saying you probably understand that I was a fabulous being in García's eyes and that he worshipped me as a good son worships a bad father. But no, this is understating it—as a dog worships its master.

"Yes, a dog, for such was García's role at my side. To keep me content, avoid a reprimand, be worthy of one of my glances—these things constituted supreme happiness for him.

"Oh, human nature is basically good! And if you doubt it, listen to the rest of my story.

"García, ten years my senior, used the formal *usted* with me.

"I used the familiar *tú* with him.

"He made my meals with the utmost solicitude.

"The leftovers were his meals.

"I, a volunteer military man, was paid 800 *reales* a month to take it easy.

"He, a drafted soldier, saved six *cuartos* a day at most, and was always working.

"I didn't pay him.

"He served me willingly, enthusiastically, devotedly.

"Such was our relationship and such was my poor orderly's superiority over me in the moral realm.

"But, nonetheless . . . for paradoxical reasons that I cannot explain . . . racial or class prejudices that corrupt our hearts? . . . I treated García harshly.

"I spoke to him only to give an order, to rebuke him for the slightest oversight or to forbid him something.

"My voice was his living command, his scourge, his torment.

"What the devil! I'm the son and brother of military men and the practice of strict obedience had ingrained in me the habit of giving strict orders.

"And after all . . . what was García? An inferior, a soldier in my company, a subordinate! An automaton! A machine!

"How much he must have suffered in his lifetime! He who loved nothing in the world as much as he loved me and never received a token of my esteem, who never heard a warm word from my lips, nor shook my hand when he left me, nor embraced me when he saw me again, nor was able to say to me, in times of danger during the war, 'Be careful, sir!' He who unfailingly loved, remained silent, and suffered in my presence, like a pariah before his god, like a eunuch before his sultana, like a slave before his owner.

"But, oh, yes! I'm sure I'm not deceiving myself, because afterward I thought about it often. If García had fallen ill, if he had wanted to leave me, if he had wept in front of me, at that very moment he would have ceased to be my inferior. I would have said to him: 'García, I can't live without seeing you.' In short, I would have realized that we were two men who at bottom loved each other . . . like brothers.

"I'm not exaggerating, my friends. Consider what an orderly is for an officer:

"When I returned to my quarters at midnight, alone, sad, upset, he would be waiting for me.

"As soon as I wanted something—at times without actually saying so—he would provide it for me.

"During a campaign he would be at my side.

"On the move he would carry me across rivers.

"In winter he would stretch out at my feet to keep them warm.

"In summer he would shelter me from the sun with the shadow of his body.

"He was the only one who knew the state of my finances.

"Only he could guess the state of my heart.

"He saw me suffer, he saw me cry; he saw me in love, weak, carried away by vices; he saw me as a callow youth; and he would look at me, feel sorry for me, and respectfully remove his cap.

"He would fight with landladies until they put my favorite dishes on the table.

"He would save from my money, that is, he would temporarily 'rob' me in order to get me out of a jam later on.

"He would check my clothes like a woman.

"He would comb my hair, brush me, dress me.

"He was, finally, protective like a father, provident like a mother, docile like a child, affectionate like a brother, economical like a wife, loyal like a friend. Like a whole family for me! My walking 'home!'

"The man had no life of his own! He lived through my life and died through my death!

"Listen.

"When the last Carlist uprising was coming to naught, I happened to be in Catalonia, under the orders of General B____.

"García was with me.

"One day we came across the enemy near the small town of Gironella.*

"From morning on we fought with great discipline, and in the evening, when victory was almost ours, we were surprised in the rear by another, and sizable, band of Carlists.

"We were caught in a crossfire!

"Seeing our hopeless position, the colonel ordered a retreat and within seconds nearly all the soldiers fled in disarray.

"But I hadn't heard the bugle call and kept fighting at the head of my company, which held the extreme right flank, and whose captain and lieutenants had been killed. I was a second lieutenant at the time.

"The Carlists advanced.

"My troops began to drop like flies all around me.

"And I didn't order a retreat.

"I was mad, prey to a fit of epilepsy, the disorder that accompanies all my passionate outbursts.

"But so pressed were those unfortunate victims of my blind rage that in the end they fled without waiting for my order, leaving most of their companions on the battlefield.

"García figured that I had ordered that flight, and ran faster than all of them thinking that perhaps I was at the head of the company.

"So I stood there, alone, saber in hand.

"And alone I advanced toward the enemy, possessed by such senseless fury that I soon fell to the ground, prey to a terrible convulsion.

"The Carlists thought I was dead and continued to pursue my fleeing men.

"Night fell without my coming to.

"The remainder of our troops were already in Gironella where they were resting and regrouping in order to pounce, the following day, on the Carlists, who had camped just outside the small town.

"García, meanwhile, had noticed my absence and decided to return to the scene of the action to recover my body, if I had died, or to help me, if I was wounded.

"To do so he had to pass through the Carlist camp.

"Only a madman or a mother would have conceived of such a reckless undertaking.

"He slipped out of the town and, making a nine-mile detour, managed to cross the enemy line.

"Shortly afterward he found me among the dead.

"I was still in the clutches of the seizure, but plunged into that strange drowsiness that lets epileptics see and hear, but not talk or move.

"García guessed on the spot what was happening to me, so he dried his tears, choked back his sobs, lifted me across his shoulders, and started toward the town.

"And he carried me like that—impassive, calm, resigned to his fate—closer and closer to the Carlists.

"He knew it, of course, but he also knew that if he didn't bring me around by the usual means or if he left me there out in the open on such a terrible windy, snowy night, I would die in a matter of hours.

"So he continued on his way.

"He had to sneak across the Carlists' lines a second time.

"The darkness of night was the only chance of salvation left to us.

"But the moon, which doesn't usually know what's happening on earth, at this point broke through its cloud barrier and appeared full, beautiful, resplendent, illuminating that entire stretch of snow-covered landscape.

"García sighed, sensing a piece of bad luck.

"I sensed it too, helpless and immobile on that martyr's back.

"What a horrendous nightmare!

"But, at the same time, what a marvel! With his burden García passed within twenty paces of a sentry without being spotted by him!

"Perhaps we would make it safely!

"But, alas, it was not to be! Fate had something else in store for us.

"The resigned Christ was reaching the end of his via dolorosa when the Carlists made him out by the light of the moon.

"'Who goes there?' challenged a voice in the distance.

"'After him!' shouted another voice closer by.

"'Holy Mother of God!' murmured García.

"And compulsively squeezing my wrists, he quickened his step.

"At this point a shot rang out and a bullet whistled.

"My orderly stopped.

"He then reeled under his heavy load, uttered a cry, and fell face downward on the ground.

"And I fell on top of him. The sacrifice was complete.

"My God, what a night!

"At first I felt García squirming and writhing under the weight of my body and inside my feeble arms.

"Then he became still.

"Afterward his limbs turned frightfully rigid.

"He was stone dead.

"I knew it but couldn't move.

"So I spent the night embracing a body . . . the body of my inferior, of my slave, of poor García.

"And that was the first time I had embraced him!

"The cool morning air revived me.

"I got to my feet and looked around.

"I was alone . . . alone among the dead.

"The Carlists had broken camp, taking all the wounded with them.

"I examined García and saw that the bullet had entered one side and gone out through the other.

"It was now my turn to carry *him,* and, shaky and unsteady, with moist eyes and a heavy heart, I entered Gironella.

"Poor García is buried there.

"For me his name is now an object of tribute and veneration.

"How many, many times I have madly asked God to allow García to be resuscitated so that I could compensate him for my asperity and violence and repay his sacrifice with love! How many times I have asked his forgiveness in my thoughts! And how his death has changed me for the better!

"Since then I've been gentle, good-natured, and solicitous of those of my inferiors who acquit themselves well, and instead of wanting them to tremble before me and consider me a being of a species superior to humans, I only want to be like a father to all of them. I've come to understand, too late, that under a soldier's coarse cloak there sometimes beats a heart that is more sublime than the one under a general's gold-trimmed uniform.

"Oh, when the orderlies I've had since then* have praised my fatherly manner; when I've heard the blessings of my company; when I've provided some solace to the sons of our native land, snatched from the bosoms of their families to serve somebody else's ambition or anger, is it not true, my poor García, that you have smiled in heaven, saying, 'My sacrifice was not in vain, as it has redeemed a number of my comrades?'"

The young officer stared up at the ceiling; we took hold of his hands and the waiter came in with the bill.

MÁLAGA, 1854

El extranjero

The Foreigner

I

"**S*TRENGTH*** does not consist of crushing one's enemy, but of mastering one's anger," says an Oriental maxim.

"Do not take unfair advantage of victory," says a book of our religion.

"Consider any guilty man who falls under your jurisdiction a miserable creature subject to the qualities of our depraved human nature, and to the extent that you are able to do so without wronging another party, show yourself merciful and lenient, for while all the attributes of God are equal, that of compassion stands out more and shines more brightly in our eyes than that of justice," Don Quijote advised Sancho Panza.*

In order to underscore all these lofty precepts, and also yield to a spirit of impartiality, we, who frequently take pleasure in relating and celebrating the heroic deeds of Spaniards during the War of Independence,* and in condemning and cursing the perfidy and cruelty of the invaders, are today going to relate an episode which, without diminishing our love of country, reinforces another no less sublime and profoundly Christian feeling—love of our fellow man, a feeling which, if because of an innate defect in humankind has to compromise with the harsh law of war, can and should shine when the enemy is crushed.

The account that follows was given to me by wholly credible individuals who participated in it up close and who are still alive. Listen to their exact words.

II

"***Good*** morning, old fellow," I said.

"God be with you, young man," he said.

"You're all alone on these roads."

"So I am. I'm coming from the mines at Linares, where I was working for several months, and I'm going to Gádor to see my family. And you?"

"I'm going to Almería, and I've come on ahead of the coach a little because I like to enjoy these beautiful April mornings. But, if I'm not mistaken, you were praying as I approached. You can continue. And in the meantime I'll go on reading since that rickety coach moves so slowly that it lets you study right in the middle of the road."

"Well, that must be some kind of story. But, what makes you think I was praying?"

"What makes me—? Because I saw you take off your hat and make the sign of the cross."

"The deuce you say! There's no use denying it. Yes, I was praying. We all have to reckon up with God."

"That's very true."

"Do you intend to walk far?"

"Me? To the inn."

"In that case, follow that path over there and we can take a shortcut."

"Gladly. The glen looks delightful. Lead the way."

And, accompanying the old man, I closed my book, left the road, and went down to a picturesque ravine.

The green hues and transparency of the distant horizon, as well as the slope of the mountain, indicated the proximity of the Mediterranean.

We walked in silence for several minutes, until the miner stopped all of a sudden.

"Exactly!" he exclaimed.

And again he took off his hat and made the sign of the cross.

We were under some leafy fig trees, by the bank of a pretty stream.

"So, old fellow," I said, sitting down on the grass. "Tell me what happened here."

"What? You know?" he asked, shuddering.

"All I know," I added very calmly, "is that a man died here. A violent death, moreover."

"You're not mistaken, young man. You're not mistaken. But, who told you?"

"Your prayers are telling me."

"That's very true. And that's why I was praying."

I looked closely at the miner's face and understood that he had always been an honest man. He was almost crying as he prayed peacefully and softly.

"Sit here, my friend," I said, offering him a cigarette.

"All right, young man. Well, thank you very much. It's on the slim side."

"Put together two of them and you'll get one twice as thick," I added, handing him a second cigarette.

"God bless you. Well, then," the old man continued, sitting down next to me, "forty-five years ago, on a morning very similar to this one, I was passing by this very spot almost at the same time."

«Forty-five years ago!» I thought to myself.

And the melancholy of time fell on my spirit. Where were the flowers of those forty-five springs? Snow-white hair on the old man's brow marked the passage of seventy winters!

When he saw that I wasn't saying anything, he struck some tinder, lighted the double cigarette, and continued as follows:

"It's quite mild. Well, sir, on the day in question I was coming from Gérgal with a load of barilla, and on reaching the point where we left the road to take this path, I came across two Spanish soldiers with a Polish prisoner in tow. This was when the first wave of Frenchmen were here, not those from 1823,* but the ones from before then."

"I understand. You mean the War of Independence."

"Right. And you weren't even born then."

"No, I wasn't."

"Oh, I see! It's written down in that book that you were reading. But mind you, the actual facts of these wars don't appear in books. Only the parts that come off best, and people believe them all religiously, needless to say. You have to be seventy years old, as I will be in the month of June, to know a thing or two. Anyway, the Pole was fighting under that rascal Napoleon, the one who's dead, because the parish priest says there's another Napoleon now. But I don't believe the new one'll come around these parts. What do you think, young man?"

"I don't know what to say."

"Why, of course. You can't have studied these things yet. The priest, who is a well-educated man, knows when we'll be rid of the Mamelukes from the East and when the Russians and Muskovites will come to Gádor to abolish the Constitution. But by then I will be dead. So let me return to the story of my Pole.

"The poor fellow had stayed behind ill in Fiñana while his fleeing companions were withdrawing toward Almería. He had a temperature, as I found out later on. An old woman was looking after him out of charity, disregarding the fact that he was an enemy—and she'll already have enjoyed many years of eternal glory for that good deed—and in spite of being compromised, she kept him hidden in her cave, near the citadel.

"It was in that lonely dwelling that two Spanish soldiers, the night before they were going to join their batallion, chanced to light their cigars with an oil lamp and discovered the poor Pole, who was lying in a corner, mumbling words in his language while delirious with fever.

"'Let's deliver him to our commanding officer,' the Spaniards agreed. 'This scoundrel will be shot tomorrow and we'll be given a commission.'

"Iwa, which was the Pole's name, as the old woman told me later on, had had tertian fever for six months and was very weak and very thin, almost consumptive.

"The good woman wept and pleaded, protesting that the foreigner couldn't go anywhere without dropping dead within a half hour.

"But she only managed to be beaten for her lack of 'patriotism.' I still haven't forgotten this word, which I had never heard spoken before.

"As for the Pole, imagine how he must've viewed that turn of events. He was prostrate from fever, and the incoherent words that he was mumbling—half Polish, half Spanish—made the two soldiers laugh.

"'Shut up, *Didón,** swine, Frog,' they said to him.

"By dint of repeated blows they dragged him from the bed.

"So as not to bore you, young man: the wretched creature walked in that condition—half naked, starving, staggering, dying—fifteen miles. Fifteen miles! Do you know how many steps there are in fifteen miles? Because that's the distance from Fiñana to here. And on foot! Barefoot! Just imagine. A well-bred man, a young man as handsome and fair as a woman, a sick man, and after six months of tertian fever, with the cycle starting over at that very moment."

"How was he able to bear it?"

"Ah! He didn't."

"Then, how did he walk fifteen miles?"

"By being jabbed with a bayonet, that's how!"

"Go on, old fellow, go on."

"I was coming along this ravine, as I usually do to shorten the trip, and they were walking on the road up above. So I stopped right here in order to observe the outcome of that atrocity while I pretended to cut a black cigar of the kind smoked back then.

"Iwa was panting like a dog going rabid. His head was bare and he was as white as a sheet, with two red spots on the upper part of his cheeks, and his eyes were blazing, but cast downward. The most pitiful sight you've ever seen.

"'*Me want die! Me kill, for God's sake!*' the foreigner was babbling with his hands clasped.

"The Spaniards laughed at that confused language and called him Frenchy, *Didón,* and other names.

"Finally, Iwa's legs buckled and he fell flat on the ground.

"I breathed again because I thought the miserable thing had passed on.

"But another bayonet jab to the shoulder made him straighten up again.

"Then he approached this ravine to jump to his death.

"As the soldiers stopped him—because it wouldn't do for their prisoner to die on them—they saw me here with my mule, which, as I've said, was loaded with barilla.

"'Hey, comrade!' they said, aiming their rifles at me. 'Bring that mule up here!'

"I obeyed without saying a word, thinking I was doing the foreigner a favor.

"'Where are you going?' they asked me when I reached the road.

"'To Almería,' I replied. 'And what you're doing is inhuman.'

"'Forget the lecture!' one of the executioners shouted.

"'A pro-French muleteer!' said the other.

"'Talk too much and you'll see what happens to you.'

"A rifle butt crashed into my chest. It was the first time I was hit by a man other than my father.

"'*No irritate! No annoy!*' the Pole exclaimed, clutching at my feet because he had fallen to the ground again.

"'Unload the barilla,' the soldiers ordered me.

"'Why?'

"'To mount this scoundrel on the mule.'

"'That's different. I'll be glad to,' I said, and I began to unload.

"'*No! No! No!*' exclaimed Iwa. '*You let them me kill!*'

"'I don't want them to kill you, you poor devil,' I said, grasping his burning hands.

"'*But me, me want! You me kill for God's sake!*'

"'You want me to kill you?'

"'*Yes, yes, good man! Suffer very much!*'

"Tears welled up in my eyes. I turned to the soldiers and spoke to them in a tone of voice that would have moved a stone:

"'Spaniards, compatriots, brothers! It's another Spaniard, who loves our country as much as any other, who's pleading with you. Leave me alone with this man.'

"'Didn't I say he was pro-French?' asked one of them.

"'You devil's muleteer,' said the other, 'watch what you're saying or I'll knock your block off!'

"'You devil's soldiers,' I responded with the same passion, 'I'm not afraid of death! You're two heartless villains. You're two strong and armed men against one unarmed foreigner with one foot in the grave. You're two cowards. Give me one of those rifles and I'll fight you until I kill you or die, but release this poor man who is ill and cannot defend himself. Oh,' I continued, seeing that one of those bullies was blushing, 'if, like me, you had sons; if you thought that tomorrow they'd find themselves in this miserable creature's homeland, in the same situation as his, alone, dying, far away from their parents; if you considered that this Pole doesn't even know what he's doing in Spain, that he's probably a conscript abducted from his family to serve the ambition of a king . . . damnation, you'd forgive him! Yes, because you're men first, Spaniards second, and this Pole is a man, a fellow man! What will Spain gain with the death of one who's suffering from tertian fever? Fight to the death against all of Napoleon's grenadiers, but let it be on the field of battle. And pardon the weak. Be generous with the conquered. Be Christians. Don't be executioners!'

"'That's enough preaching,' said the one who always took the lead in cruelty, the one who forced Iwa to march at the point of a bayonet, the one who wanted to buy a commission at the expense of Iwa's corpse.

"'What should we do, mate?' asked the other soldier, half moved by my words.

"'It's very simple,' replied the first one. 'Watch.'

"And without giving me time to anticipate his movements, let alone to prevent them, he shot the Pole in the heart.

"Iwa looked at me tenderly, I don't know whether before or after dying.

"That look promised me heaven, where perhaps the martyr already was.

"Immediately afterward the two soldiers gave me a beating with the ramrods of their rifles.

"The one who had killed the foreigner cut off one of his ears and put it in his pocket. It was verification for the commission that he wanted.

"Afterwards he stripped Iwa and robbed him, even taking a certain locket—with a picture of a woman or a female saint—that he wore around his neck. Then they set out for Almería.

"I buried Iwa in this ravine, there, where you're sitting, and went back to Gérgal because I realized that I wasn't well. As a matter of fact, that incident gave rise to a terrible illness that landed me at death's door."

"And you never again saw those soldiers? You don't know their names?"

"No, sir, but from the description that I was later given by the old woman who cared for the Pole, I found out that one of those Spaniards was nicknamed *Risas,** and that he was in fact the one who had killed and robbed the poor foreigner."

At this point the coach caught up with us. The old man and I went up to the road, shook hands, and said goodbye, pleased that we had met. We had shed tears together!

III

Three nights later I was having coffee with several friends at Almería's exquisite casino.

Near us, at another table, were two old men, retired army officers—one a major, the other a colonel, according to somebody who knew them.

We could not avoid overhearing their conversation because they were speaking loudly, like men who are accustomed to giving orders.

All of a sudden two of the colonel's words reached my ears and attracted my attention:

"Poor *Risas* . . ."

"Risas!" I exclaimed to myself. And I began to listen intentionally.

"Poor *Risas*," the colonel was saying, "was taken prisoner by the

French when they conquered Málaga, and, after numerous stops, ended up in Sweden no less, where I too was being held captive, like everybody else who didn't manage to escape with the Marquis of La Romana. I met him there because he became friendly with Juan, my lifelong orderly, or career-long orderly, and when Napoleon was so cruel as to take to Russia, forming a part of his Grande Armée, all of us Spaniards who were his prisoners, I took *Risas* as an aide. Then I found out that he was scared stiff of Poles, or superstitiously terrified of Poland, because all he did was ask Juan and me 'if we'd have to pass through there to get to Russia,' shuddering at the idea that it could become a reality. Unquestionably, that man, whose mind had been affected by his abuse of alcoholic drinks, but who otherwise was a good soldier and a middling cook, had had something serious happen to him with some Pole, either in the war in Spain or in his long journey through other countries.

"Upon arriving in Warsaw, where we laid over for several days, *Risas* fell gravely ill with brain fever as a result of the panic that gripped him after we had entered Poland, and I, pretty fond of him by then, balked at leaving him there alone when we received our marching orders. So my commanding officers gave me permission to have Juan stay behind in Warsaw to care for him, with the understanding, once the crisis was resolved one way or another, that he, Juan, would come in search of me with one of the many supply convoys that would follow that great swarm of people with my regiment in the vanguard. Imagine, then, my surprise when the very day that we set out, and just a few hours after having begun to march, my former orderly showed up, terror-stricken, and told me what had just happened to poor *Risas*. I'm telling you it's the most singular and amazing thing that's ever occurred. Listen to me and you'll see if there's a reason I haven't forgotten this story in forty-two years.

"Juan had found good lodgings to take care of *Risas* in the home of a certain peasant woman, a widow with three marriageable daughters. And as soon as we Spaniards arrived in Warsaw, she began asking us, through French interpreters, if we knew anything about a son of hers named Iwa who had gone to the war in Spain in 1808; it had been three years since she'd had any news at all, which was not the case with other families whose sons had been conscripted. As Juan was such a wheedler, he found a way to console and give hope to that unfortunate mother, which was why, in return, she offered to care for *Risas* on seeing him fall ill, in her presence, with brain fever. Now: when the good woman was helping to undress the patient, Juan saw her turn pale all of a sudden and convulsively seize a certain silver locket with an image or portrait in miniature, which *Risas* always wore around his neck, under his clothes, as a kind of talisman or magical charm against the Poles because he thought it represented a Virgin or Saint of that country.

"'Iwa! Iwa!' the widow then screamed in a horrible voice, shaking *Risas,* who didn't understand a thing, lethargic as he was from the fever.

"At this point the daughters came in, and, informed of what had happened, took the locket and held it alongside their mother's face, catching Juan's eye and indicating through sign language that he should look at both. Which he did, and he saw that the image was a portrait of the mother. Confronting him, then, inasmuch as his compatriot couldn't answer them, they began to ask him a thousand questions with unintelligible words, although with gestures and movements that clearly revealed the most ominous fury. Juan shrugged his shoulders, using sign language of his own to imply that he knew nothing about the source of that portrait and that he hadn't known *Risas* all that long. The honest face of my trustworthy orderly must have convinced those four infuriated lionesses that the poor fellow wasn't at fault. Besides, *he* wasn't wearing the locket. But the other one . . . they killed the other one. They beat and clawed poor *Risas* to death. And that's all I know about this drama because I've never been able to find out why *Risas* had that portrait."

"Allow me to tell you," I chimed in, unable to restrain myself.

And after being introduced to the colonel and major by my friends, I approached their table and told all of them the miner's frightful story.

As soon as I finished, the major, a man in his seventies, exclaimed with the simple faith of a one-time soldier, with the impulse of a good Spaniard, and with all the authority of his age:

"As God lives, gentlemen, there's more than happenstance at work here!"

ALMERÍA, 1854

El afrancesado

The French Sympathizer

I

AROUND the year 1808, in the small village of Padrón, which is in the province of Galicia, there lived a certain García de Paredes who in the guise of being a reliable druggist sold all sorts of palliatives and useless cures. He was an unmarried old misanthrope, reputed to be and probably was, a descendant of the famous man who could slay a bull with a single blow of his fist.*

It was a cold, gloomy fall night. The sky was cloaked with thick clouds, and the total absence of artificial illumination allowed the darkness to blanket all the streets and squares of the village.

At approximately ten o'clock on that terrible night, a night made even more ominous by the dismal circumstances of the motherland, there came out on the square that today is named Constitution a silent group of shadows, even blacker than the darkness of sky and land, that advanced toward García de Paredes' apothecary, which had been all closed up since Vespers, that is, from exactly eight-thirty.

"What'll we do?" asked one of the shadows in flawless Galician.

"Nobody has seen us," observed another.

"Break the door down!" one woman proposed.

"And kill all of them!" muttered as many as fifteen voices.

"I'll take care of the druggist!" one of the boys exclaimed.

"We'll all take care of that one!"

"For being a rat!"

"For being a collaborator!"

"I hear that more than twenty Frenchmen are dining with him tonight."

"I'm not surprised! Since they know that they're safe with him a great many have come!"

"Ah! If it were in my house! I've thrown three of the soldiers billeted with me down the well!"

"Yesterday my wife slashed the throat of one of them!"

"And I," said a friar in a deep voice, "I've asphyxiated two captains by leaving ignited coal in their cell, which used to be mine!"

"And that infamous druggist has befriended them!"

"How he played up to those excommunicated good-for-nothings while out walking with them yesterday!"

"Who would have expected it from García de Paredes. Not even a month ago he was the most courageous, the most patriotic, the most fervent royalist supporter in the town!"

"Why, he used to sell portraits of Prince Ferdinand in his apothecary!"

"And now he sells them of Napoleon!"

"Before, he stirred us to fight against the invaders."

"And since they came to Padrón he's gone over to their side!"

"And tonight he's serving dinner to all the officers!"

"Listen to the racket they're making. They're shouting 'Long live the Emperor!'"

"Patience," muttered the friar. "It's still very early."

"Let's allow them to get drunk," an old woman declared. "Then we go in . . . and not one of them will escape alive."

"I demand that the druggist be quartered!"

"He'll be cut up in eighths if you wish! A French sympathizer is more odious than a Frenchman. The Frenchman tramples a foreign people; the French sympathizer betrays and dishonors his native country. The Frenchman commits an assassination; the French sympathizer, parricide!"

II

While the preceding scene was taking place at the door of the apothecary shop, García de Paredes and his guests were upstairs enjoying the most outrageous feast that you can imagine.

There were, in effect, twenty Frenchmen whom the druggist had invited to his table, all of them officers and commanders.

García de Paredes was about forty-five years old; he was tall, lean and yellower than a mummy—it could be said that his skin had been dead for a long time; his forehead extended all the way to his nape thanks to a clear, shiny bald spot whose luster had something phosphoric about it; his eyes, black and dull, sunk in bony sockets, resembled those lagoons contained between mountains that only offer darkness, vertigo, and death to those who look at them, lagoons that reflect nothing; that roar dully on occasion, but without changing, that devour everything that falls on their surfaces; that return nothing; that nobody has been able to fathom; that are not fed by any river, and whose depths seek their imagination in the antipodal seas.

The supper was abundant, the wine good, the conversation cheerful and animated.

The Frenchmen laughed, swore, blasphemed, sang, smoked, ate, and drank all at the same time.

This one related Napoleon's secret loves; that one, the night of May 2nd in Madrid;* someone else, the Battle of the Pyramids;* yet another, the execution of Louis XVI.

García de Paredes drank, laughed, and talked as much as the others, or perhaps more than any other; and so eloquent had he been on behalf of the imperial cause that the soldiers of Napoleon had embraced him, applauded, and improvised hymns to him.

"Gentlemen!" the druggist said. "The war that we Spaniards carry on against you is as foolish as it is unnecessary. You, sons of the Revolution, come to Spain to rid it of its traditional abjections, to free it from prejudice, to dissipate religious darkness, to improve its antiquated customs, to teach us those highly useful and incontestable truths that there is no God, that there is no afterlife, that penance, fasting, chastity, and other Catholic virtues are quixotic fantasies unsuited to a civilized people, and that Napoleon is the true Messiah, the redeemer of peoples, the friend of humankind. Gentlemen! May the Emperor live as long as I hope he lives!"

"Bravo, hurrah!" exclaimed the men of the second of May.

The druggist bowed his head in unspeakable anguish.

He soon raised it again, as steady and as serene as before.

He drank a glass of wine and continued:

"An ancestor of mine, also a García de Paredes, a barbarian, a Samson, a Hercules, a Milo* from Crotona, killed two hundred Frenchmen in one day. I believe it was in Italy. You can see that he wasn't as much of a French sympathizer as I am! He trained in combat against the Moors of the kingdom of Granada; he was knighted by the Catholic King himself, and more than once mounted guard at the Quirinal, our kinsman Alexander Borgia being Pope!

You didn't think I was of such high lineage, did you! Well, this Diego García de Paredes, this ancestor of mine, who has had as his descendant a druggist, seized Conseza and Manfredonia, took Cerinola by storm and fought courageously in the Battle of Pavia. There we took prisoner a king of France whose sword had been in Madrid about three centuries until that innkeeper's son who is at your head, and whose name is Murat, stole it from us three months ago."

At this point the druggist paused again. Some Frenchmen showed that they wanted to respond; but, getting up and imposing silence on all of them by his attitude, he grasped convulsively a glass and exclaimed in a thundering voice:

"A toast, gentlemen, that my ancestor, who was an animal, be damned, and that right now he be in the depths of hell! Long live the French of Francis I and Napoleon Bonaparte!"

"Long may they live!" responded the invaders, considering themselves satisfied.

And they all drained their glasses.

At this point the sound of voices was heard in the street, or rather, at the door of the apothecary.

"Did you hear?" the Frenchmen asked.

García de Paredes smiled.

"They're probably coming to kill me!" he said.

"Who?"

"The people of Padrón."

"Why?"

"For being a French sympathizer! They've been coming around my house for several nights. But why should it concern us? Let's continue our celebration."

"Yes, let's continue!" the guests exclaimed. "We'll defend you!"

And clinking bottles rather than glasses,

"Long live Napoleon! Death to Ferdinand! Death to Galicia!" they cried in unison.

García de Paredes waited for the toasting to conclude, then called in a lugubrious tone:

"Celedonio!"

The apothecary's clerk stuck his pale and rattled head through a small doorway without daring to come all the way inside the room.

"Celedonio, bring paper and an inkwell," the druggist said calmly.

The clerk returned with writing materials.

"Sit down!" his master continued. "Now write down the numbers that I give you. Divide them into two columns. At the top of the right-hand column put *Debit,* and at the top of the other, *Credit.*"

"Sir," the clerk stammered. "There's some kind of riot going on outside. They're shouting *Death to the druggist!* And they want to come in!"

"Be quiet and leave them alone! Just do as you've been told."

The Frenchmen laughed in amazement when they saw the druggist busying himself settling accounts while threatened by ruin and death.

Celedonio raised his head and, his pen at the ready, waited to write down the numbers.

"Let's see, gentlemen," García de Paredes then said, addressing his table companions. "It's a question of summing up our celebration in a single toast. Let's go down the table in order. You, Captain, tell me—how many Spaniards do you suppose you've killed since crossing the Pyrenees?"

"Bravo! Magnificent idea!" exclaimed the Frenchmen.

"I . . . ," the questioned party said, leaning back in his chair and twisting his mustache insolently. "I . . . I've probably killed . . . personally . . . with my sword . . . put down ten or twelve!"

"Eleven to the right!" the druggist shouted, addressing his clerk.

The clerk repeated, after writing:

"*Debit,* eleven."

"Right!" the host continued. "Now you—I'm speaking to you, master Julio."

"Me . . . six."

"And you, Major?"

"Me . . . twenty."

"I . . . eight."

"I . . . fourteen."

"I . . . none."

"I don't know! I've fired blindly," answered each one as his turn came.

And the clerk continued putting down numbers in the right-hand column.

"Let's see now, Captain," García de Paredes went on. "Let's begin again with you. How many Spaniards do you hope to kill in the rest of the war, assuming that it'll last, say . . . three more years?"

"Eh!," the Captain responded. "Who can figure out something like that?"

"Take a guess. I implore you."

"Put down another eleven."

"Eleven to the left," García de Paredes dictated.

And Celedonio repeated:

"*Credit,* eleven."

"And you?" the druggist asked in the same order followed previously.

"I . . . fifteen."

"I . . . twenty."

"I . . . one hundred."

"I . . . one thousand," went the replies.

"Put down ten for each of them, Celedonio," the druggist said sardonically. "Now, add the two columns separately."

The poor young man, who had written the numbers trembling with fear, was forced to do the addition counting on his fingers as old women do. Such was his terror.

After a period of ominous silence, he exclaimed to his master:

"*Debit,* 285. *Credit,* 200."

"Which is to say," García de Paredes added, "two hundred eighty-five *dead,* and two hundred sentenced to death! In all, four hundred eighty-five *victims!*"

And he pronounced these words in such a deep, hollow voice that the Frenchmen looked at each other in alarm.

In the meantime the druggist was totaling another account.

"We're truly heroes!" he exclaimed on finishing it. "We have drunk seventy bottles, that is, a little more than thirteen gallons of wine, which, divided by twenty-one, because we've all drunk liberally, comes out to a little over half a gallon per head. I repeat, we're a bunch of heroes!"

At this point the people of Padrón were breaking down the door of the apothecary shop, and the clerk, shaking from fright, stammered:

"They're coming in!"

"What time is it?" the druggist asked quite calmly.

"Eleven o'clock. But, can't you hear them coming in?"

"Let them. The time has come."

"Time! Time for what?" the Frenchmen mumbled, attempting to get up.

But they were so drunk that they could not move out of their chairs.

"Let them in! Let them in!" they nevertheless cried in drunken voices, pulling out their sabers with much difficulty, unable to stand up. "Let the dogs come in! We'll give them a reception!"

Up the stairway came the sound of glass crashing as the people of Padrón went about breaking up the jars and phials in the shop, while one unanimous, terrible cry was heard:

"Death to the French sympathizer!"

III

Hearing such an outcry inside his home, García de Paredes jumped up as if propelled by a spring and leaned against the table in order not to fall back in the chair. He glanced all about with a look of incredible joy on his face, his lips showing the immortal smile of the victor, and thus, transfigured and radiant, with a double tremor both of death and enthusiasm, he pronounced the following words, intermittent and solemn like a death knell:

"Frenchmen! If any of you, or all of you together, found a propitious occasion to avenge the deaths of two hundred and eighty-five compatriots and to save the lives of two hundred more; if by sacrificing your lives you could allay the anger of the indignant spirit of your ancestors, punish the executioners of two hundred and eighty-five heroes and deliver from death two hundred companions, two hundred brothers, and thus increase the partisans of your motherland's army by two hundred champions of national independence, would you consider for even a moment your own miserable life? Would you hesitate an instant to embrace, like Samson, the column of the temple, and to die at the cost of killing the enemies of God?"

"What is he saying?" the Frenchmen asked each other.

"Sir, the murderers are coming into the hall!" Celedonio cried.

"Let them come!" shouted García de Paredes. "Open the door for them. Let all of them come—so they can see how a descendant of the soldier who fought at Pavia dies!"

The Frenchmen, terrified, stupefied, glued to their chairs by an oppressive lethargy and believing that the death of which the Spaniard spoke was going to enter the room behind the insurgents, made arduous efforts to raise the sabers which lay on the table; but they did not even succeed in getting their fingers to grasp the hilts: it seemed as if the iron pieces were stuck to the table by an insuperable force of attraction.

At this point more than fifty men and women burst into the room armed with clubs, daggers and pistols, yelling wildly, their eyes blazing.

"Death to all!" exclaimed several women, the first ones to rush forth.

"Stop!" shouted García de Paredes with such a voice, with such an attitude, with such an expression on his face, that this shout, combined with the immobility and silence of the twenty Frenchmen, imposed a cold terror on the mob, which was not expecting so calm and gloomy a welcome.

"You have no need to brandish your daggers," the druggist continued in a faint voice. "I've done more than all of you on behalf of the independence of our native land. I've pretended to be a French sympathizer! And, you already see! The twenty enemy officers and commanders, all twenty! Don't touch them—they're dying of poison!"

The Spaniards let out a simultaneous shout of terror and admiration. They took another step in the direction of the guests and found that the majority of them were already dead, their heads slumped forward, their arms stretched out on the table, and their hands rigid on the hilts of their sabers. The others were dying silently.

"Long live García de Paredes!" the Spaniards then exclaimed, surrounding the dying hero.

"Celedonio," the druggist muttered. "We've run out of opium. Order more opium from La Coruña."

And he fell to his knees.

Only then did the people of Padrón understand that the druggist also was poisoned.

You would have seen then a scene that was as sublime as it was terrible. Several women, seated on the floor, supported in their laps and arms the expiring patriot; now they were the first ones in showering him with caresses and blessings as before they had been the first ones in demanding his death. The men had gathered all the lights from the table and, kneeling down, illuminated this group bound by patriotism and love. And in the shadows there were, finally, the twenty dead or dying men, some of whom were falling from their chairs with a heavy, terrible noise.

Hearing the sighs of death as one after another of the Frenchmen dropped to the floor, a glorious smile illuminated the face of García de Paredes, who shortly afterwards passed away, blessed by a minister of the Lord and mourned by his fellow patriots.

MADRID, 1856

¡Viva el papa!

"Long Live the Pope!"

I

THE moving episode that I'm going to relate is absolutely historical, like the previous ones and the following ones,* and not just because of the subject matter, but because of the form as well. The person who's going to tell it is still alive, and mind you, I'm not that person—the narrator is a retired captain who left active service in 1814.

Today I will not be a writer, just a mere amanuensis. So I ask of you neither admiration nor indulgence, only that you believe me without reservation.

As invention the subject is of little importance, but then it belongs to a genre in which I wouldn't take the trouble to invent anything.

I consider myself a liberal, and a poor retired captain has moved me deeply by recounting the political problems of a very absolutist pope.

My aim is to move you today with the same account so that the number of the defeated can attentuate my own defeat.

If I succeed in so doing, I'll be able to exclaim like the adulteress: "Let him who is without sin call me . . . neo-Catholic."

I yield to my captain.

II

"**On** one of the hottest days of the month of July, 1809—and believe me, it was hot that year—around ten o'clock in the morning, we entered Montelimart, a town or village in Dauphiné. I don't know what it is, I've never known, and I certainly didn't need to know that such a thing as France existed in the world."

"Oh! So it was in France?"

"Well, naturally! Where else is the Dauphiné going to be except in France? And don't think that it was right at the border. It was considerably inland, closer to Piedmont than Spain—"

"Continue, Captain. Let the children learn in school. And you, Eduardito, let's see if you can quiet down."

"Well, as I was saying, we entered Montelimart, suffocating from the heat and dust and exhausted from walking for three weeks, twenty-seven of us, Spanish officers who had been taken prisoner in Gerona.* But don't think that it was in the surrender of the fortress—no, it was in a sally we made a few days earlier to block fortifications at the French encampment. Although this is neither here nor there. The point is that they captured us and took us to Perpignan, and from there to Dijon. And that's the reason for what I'm going to relate.

"Well, sir, as one becomes accustomed to everything, and the emperor allotted us ten *reales* a day during the trip—which we were making in marches of ten or twelve miles—and no one was guarding us, because each of us had pledged with a nod of the head that the others would not desert, and twenty-seven Spaniards together have never gotten bored, it turned out that despite the heat, fatigue, and not knowing a single word of French, we had some enjoyable times, especially from eleven in the morning to seven in the afternoon, when we would stay in towns along our route, because we marched at night inasmuch as it was cooler.

"Antonio, give me a light for my pipe, will you?

"Montelimart! What a pretty town! The café is on a street near the square, and we went inside to cool off, that is, to escape the sun—because we didn't have enough money to treat ourselves—while three of the group went to see the prefect to obtain the billeting slips that in France are called *mandats*.

"I don't know if the café is still as it was back then. Forty-four years have gone by! I remember that to the left of the door there was a window covered by a grille and in front a table at which some of us officers sat down. One of them was C____, Almería's parliamentary deputy, who died last year. You see that what I'm telling you can be confirmed."

"But aren't you saying he's dead?"

"Well, I'm assuming that C____ must have told his family," replied the captain, tamping his pipe with his fingernail.

"You're right, Captain. Continue. Pay no attention to these doubting Thomases."

"Well stated, my son. So: as I was saying, we were sitting at the table when we heard loud shouting and saw a lot of people running along the street, but since the shouting was in French we didn't understand it.

"'*Le Pape! Le Pape! Le Pape!*' the women and children cried out again and again, their hands raised to the sky. Meanwhile, all the balconies were opening and filling with people, and the waiters and a few villagers who were shooting pool ran outside, their mouths wide open as if they'd heard that the sun had come to a standstill."

"Well, it *is* standing still, Gramps!"

"Mind your manners and be quiet when your elders are speaking!"

"Pay no attention, Captain. These kids nowadays. . . ."

"Sure, but it *is* standing still," the boy mumbled.

"'*Le Pape! Le Pape!* What does that mean?' we all asked each other. And we stopped one of the waiters in the café and managed to convey our lack of comprehension.

"The waiter took two keys and with his hands outlined a kind of morion on his head; then he sat on a chair and said:

"'*Le Pontife!*'

"'Ah!', said C____, who was the quickest of us all, which explains why later he became a parliamentary deputy. 'The pontiff! The pope!'

"'*Oui, monsieur. Le Pape! Pie sept!*'

"'Pius VII! The pope!' we exclaimed, without daring to believe what we were hearing. 'What's the pope doing in France? Because isn't the pope in Rome? Do popes travel? The pope in Montelimart?'

"Don't wonder at our amazement, my friends. Back then everything had more prestige than nowadays. Travel wasn't as easy, nor were there as many newspapers. I think that in all of Spain only one was being published, and it was the size of a tax receipt. The pope for us was a supernatural being, not a man of flesh and blood. In the whole world there was only one pope, and at that time the world was much bigger than it is today, and full of mysteries, unknown parts, and unexplored continents. Furthermore, there still sounded in our ears our mothers' and teachers' words: 'The pope is the Vicar of Christ, his representative on earth, an infallible authority, and whatever he binds on earth shall be bound in heaven, and whatever he looses on earth shall be loosed in heaven.'

"I think I've made myself clear. I think you understand all the respect, all the veneration, all the alarm that we poor Spaniards from that bygone century experienced on hearing that His Holiness the pope was in a small French town and that we were going to see him.

"Sure enough: no sooner did we leave the café than we noticed in the square—which, as I've told you, was nearby—a dusty post chaise stopped in front of an ordinary-looking house, guarded by two cavalrymen whose drawn sabers glanced in the sunlight.

"There were more than five hundred people milling around and inspecting the coach with keen curiosity, unhindered by the guards who, on the other hand, did not permit the crowd to go near the door of that house where Pius VII had alighted while the team of horses was being changed."

"And what house was that, Grandpa? The mayor's?"

"No, my son. It was the diligence relay station.

"Seeing that we were military officers, the guards accorded us a little more respect and allowed us to go right up to the door, but not pass beyond the threshold.

"At any rate, we managed to see very clearly two figures who occupied one of the corners of that hall or doorway.

"Two elderly men—what am I saying? Two *decrepit* old men soaked with perspiration and covered with dust, overcome with fatigue, suffocating from the heat, scarcely breathing, were drinking water from a glass which they passed back and forth. They were sitting on old, rush-bottomed chairs. Their ankle-length cassocks, one white, the other purple, were so dirty and rumpled as a result of their long journey that they looked more like the humble tunics of pilgrims than the ostentatious habits of princes of the church.

"No distinguishing emblem revealed to us which one was Pius VII—because we were in the dark when it came to popes' and cardinals' robes—but we all exclaimed at the same time:

"'The taller one! The one in white!'

"And do you know why we said that? Because his companion was crying and he wasn't; because his calmness revealed that he was a martyr; because his humility showed that he was a king.

"As for his figure—I have the impression I'm still seeing it. Picture a man in his seventies, skinny, tall, and somewhat stooped from age. His face, creased by several deep wrinkles, revealed the most austere energy, but energy softened by kind lips which seemed to flow with persuasion and consolation. His grave nose, his peaceful eyes—shriveled over the years—and a few hairs as white as snow, inspired at once reverence and trust. Only when looking at the face of my dear father and at those of saints to whom I prayed had I experienced up to then emotion of that sort.

"The priest who accompanied His Holiness was also very aged, and in his face, contracted by pain and indignation, one discerned a man of profound thought and quick, decisive action. He looked more like a general than an apostle.

"But, was what we were seeing really so? The pontiff under arrest, journeying in the worst part of the summer, with the sun at its hottest, in the company of two ill-mannered guards, attended by just one priest, with no other lodgings than the hall of a diligence relay station, no other pillow than a wood chair?

"In such an extraordinary case, in such a monstrous outrage, in such a terrible drama, only one man could have intervened, one who was more extraordinary, more monstrous, and more terrible than all that we were seeing. The name *Napoleon* was on our lips. Napoleon had marched us inside France too! Napoleon had turned the East upside down, made war on our native land, toppled all the thrones of Europe! He had to have been the one who snatched the pope from the chair of Saint Peter and paraded him like that throughout the French empire, as the Jews paraded the Redeemer through the streets before he was crucified!

"But what was the fate of the blessed prisoner? What had happened in Rome? Was there a new religion in the south of Europe? Was Napoleon pope?

"We didn't know what to make of it and, if the truth be told, I myself never did learn a thing."

"Well, Captain, if I may interject a quick clarification, it will cap your remarkable story and attest its importance."

III

"On the 17th of May of that same year 1809, Napoleon issued a decree by which he annexed the papal states to the French empire, declaring Rome a 'free imperial city.'

"The Roman people didn't dare protest against this measure, but the pope resisted it passively from his Quirinal palace, where he could still rely on several authorities and his Swiss Guard.

"It happened then that some fishermen on the Tiber River caught a sturgeon, and they wanted to give it to Saint Peter's successor as a gift. The French seized the opportunity to take the last step against the authority of Pius VII and shouted: 'To arms!' The cannon of Sant-Angelo proclaimed the extinction of the temporal government of the popes and the tricolor flag flew over the Vatican.

"The Secretary of State, Cardinal Pacca (who, undoubtedly, was the priest that you saw with Pius VII), hurried to His Holiness's side and, when the two elderly men saw each other, they exclaimed: '*Consummatum est!*'*

"Indeed, while the pope was uttering his final excommunication against them, the invaders were penetrating the Quirinal, battering doors down with axes.

"In the Sanctification Room they encountered forty Swiss guards, the remnant of the power of the ex-king of Rome, who let them in because His Holiness had directed that no resistance at all be offered.

"General Radet, in command of the wreckers, found the pope in the regular Audience Room surrounded by Cardinals Pacca and Despuig and several clerks from the secretary's office.

"Pius VII was wearing a rochet and a mozzetta and had left his bed to receive the enemy; he appeared to be amazingly calm.

"It was midnight. Radet, deeply moved, didn't dare to speak. Finally, he conveyed to His Holiness the order that he renounce the temporal government of the Roman states. The pope answered that he could not do that because they were not his, but the Church's, and he was made their administrator by the will of Heaven. General Radet replied by showing the pope the order to take him prisoner to France.

"At dawn the following day Pius VII left his palace escorted by constables and gendarmes, hopping over the debris of the doors, accompanied only by Cardinal Pacca, his sole token of worldly splendor a *papetto*—a coin equivalent to one peseta—which he carried in his pocket.

"On the outskirts of the Popolo gate a post chaise was awaiting the pope; they made him get in and then locked the doors with a key, which Radet handed over to the cavalry guard.

"The shutters on the right, where the pope sat, were nailed shut so that he couldn't be seen."

IV

"***And*** I came across him in that post chaise! Now you know I'm not lying!"

"You're right to interrupt me, Captain, because I've finished and we want to hear the rest from you."

"Well, here it is, my friends.

"I was saying that Pius VII and Cardinal Pacca—I'm delighted to have learned his name!—were sitting in the hall of the diligence relay station, that people had gathered in the street, that the guards were holding them back, and that we Spaniards had managed to get so close to the door that we saw the two august priests very clearly.

"Pius VII fixed his eyes on us by chance and undoubtedly realized, from our strange and torn uniforms, that we too were foreigners and captives of Napoleon. At any rate, after saying a few words to the cardinal, he gazed intently at us for a long time.

"At this point a fandango broke out nearby, wonderfully played and sung by our three companions who were returning with the billeting slips.

"I think I told you that we had bought two guitars before leaving Catalonia, and if I've forgotten to tell you, I'm telling you now.

"Upon hearing that music and the accompanying lyrics, the pope raised his head again and looked at us with greater interest and tenderness.

"The Italian, the musician, had recognized the singing.

"He knew that we were Spaniards!

"Being a Spaniard back then meant much more than it does nowadays. It meant being the conqueror of the Captain of the Century; being a soldier at Bailén and Zaragoza; being a defender of history, of tradition, and of the ancient faith; guardian of the independence of nations; champion of Christ; crusader for freedom. On this last point we were greatly mistaken. But who would have guessed then, as we defended Don Fernando VII against the French, that this very king would *summon* them after fourteen years and *bring* them to Spain to fight against us, as he did in 1823? In short, I don't want to say more because there are some things that still make my blood boil.

"Picking up the thread of my story, then. A saintly blush covered the pope's face when he pondered our misfortune and remembered the examples of heroism that Spain was giving to the world, and the purest enthusiasm sparkled in his loving eyes, eyes that seemed to be full of affection for us.

"For our part, understanding as we did all the partiality that His Holiness was showing us at that moment, we tried to represent to him, through expressions and gestures, our veneration and devotion, as well as the pain and indignation that we felt on seeing him under arrest and mistreated by his corrupt children. Almost instinctively we removed our helmets—which really startled the French, who wore their shakos pulled tightly down—and placed our right hands over our hearts like someone who's making a profession of faith.

"The pope raised his eyes to heaven and began to pray. He knew that his blessing could bring down upon us the anger of the ungodly townspeople who surrounded us, as we knew that a shout of 'Long live the pope!' could aggravate his own situation. How proud the Frenchmen who surrounded us were on seeing that supreme triumph of the Revolution over authority! How great they thought France was at that moment!

At this point the crowd separated and there appeared in the space that had been cleared by the guards a woman from the town, much older than the pontiff—a neat, poorly dressed centenarian, her hair as white as snow, shaking from age and excitement, stooped, suppliant, carrying in her hands a wicker basket full of peaches whose red and golden hues could be seen under the green leaves with which they were covered.

"The guards tried to stop her, but she looked at them so meekly, her attitude was so inoffensive, her gift was so tender and loving, her age inspired so much respect, there was such trust in that act of piety, and that last century, in short, faithful to its beliefs, meant so much by coming to welcome the Vicar of Christ in the middle of his Street of Bitterness that the soldiers of the Revolution and the Empire understood or sensed that that anachronism, that charitableness from another time, that peaceable and defenseless heart that had survived the guillotine by chance in no way diminished or tarnished the triumphs of the conqueror of Europe, and they allowed the poor woman to enter that fortunate hall, which reminded us of another fortunate place where some simple shepherds also made an offering to the Son of God incarnate.

"An interesting scene then took place between the Christian woman and the pontiff.

"She knelt and, without saying a word, presented the basket of fruit to the august prisoner.

"Pius VII wiped with his blessed hands the tears that were rolling down her old face, and when she bent to kiss his foot, the Holy Father placed one hand on her bowed head and raised the other to heaven with the inspired pose of a prophet.

"'*¡Viva el papa!*' we then exclaimed in our Spanish language, unable to control ourselves.

"And we entered the hall resolved to do or die.

"Pius VII stood when he heard the shout and, extending his hands in our direction, stopped us, as if his majestic pose had overwhelmed us. So we fell to our knees and the Holy Father blessed us once, twice, and then a third time.

"At the same instant there arose in the doorway and in the entire square something like a hurricane of shouts, and we turned around horrified, thinking that the French were threatening His Holiness. The least of it was that they would be threatening us! We were prepared to die!

"But imagine our astonishment on seeing that the guards, the men of the town, the women, the children—all of Montelimart!—were on their knees, with their heads uncovered and tears in their eyes, exclaiming:

"'*Vive le Pape!*'

"At this point the people ignored the order to stay back, overran the hall, and asked the pontiff's blessing.

"Pius VII took one of the green leaves that covered the basket of peaches that the old woman continued offering him, put it to his lips, and kissed it.

"The crowd for its part seized the pieces of fruit as if they were relics; everybody embraced the poor woman; the pope, trembling from emotion, passed through the multitude, blessed us once more, and got in the post chaise. And the guards, ashamed at what had just happened, gave the order to leave.

"As for us, throughout that whole day we weren't prisoners of war in France, but guests of peace.

"And that's the end of the story."

V

"There's one more thing!" exclaimed the same man who had earlier given an account of the events in Rome. "Listen to me for a moment.

"In 1814, five years after the story told by the captain, the strength of public opinion in all of France forced Napoleon to set Pius VII free.

"So His Holiness returned along the same road where he had been seen by the Spanish prisoners, and here is how Chateaubriand describes the send-off that France gave to the successor of Saint Peter:

"'Pius VII journeyed in the midst of songs and tears, the pealing of bells and shouts of *Long live the pope!, Long live the head of the church!* The only ones who remained in the towns were those who couldn't walk, and pilgrims spent nights out in the country waiting for the arrival of the elderly priest. SUCH IS, OVER THE POWER OF THE AX AND THE SCEPTER, THE SUPERIORITY OF THE STRENGTH OF THE WEAK SUPPORTED BY RELIGION AND MISFORTUNE.'"

GUADIX, 1857

El carbonero alcalde

The Mayor of Lapeza*

I

ANOTHER day I'll narrate the tragic events that preceded the entrance of the French into the Moorish city of Guadix in order to describe how its incensed inhabitants beat and killed the chief magistrate, Don Francisco Trujillo, who had been accused of not having dared to go out to face Napoleon's army with the three hundred compatriots that he could have had at his command—compatriots armed with shotguns, sabers, knives, and slings.

Today, with no other aim than to indicate where matters stood when the sublime episode that I'm going to relate occurred, I'll say that the Captain General of Granada was, as the French sympathizers called him, His Excellency Count Horacio Sebastiani, and the Governor of the District of Guadix was General Godinot, successor to the Colonel of Dragoons, 20th cavalry regiment, Monsieur Corvineau, who had had the glory of occupying the city on 16 February 1810.

Two months had passed since that abhorred date, and Napoleon's troops held such sway over Guadix that that classic land of rebels and guerrilla fighters was as quiet as a cemetery. Only from time to time did one see a good patriot hanging from the balconies of town halls, and there was less and less surprise surrounding certain mysterious "casualties" in the invading army, produced, as everyone knows, because the citizens of Guadix, like many other Spaniards, took to throwing their billeted military down wells. People were beginning to speak broken French, and even children knew how to say *Didón* to refer to the conquerors, which was a clear indication that the assimilation of Spaniards and Frenchmen was progressing considerably, causing the latter to hope for a quick alliance between both nations. Our grandmothers were already dancing (that is to say, the grandmothers of the grandchildren of French-sympathizer bigshots, not mine, thank heaven), they were already dancing, I started to say, with the victorious officers of Marengo, Austerlitz, and Wagram, and there was even an instance of a carefree beauty in ornamental comb and long, tightfitting dress, which was the height of elegance at that time, who had looked favorably at one or another grenadier, dragoon, or hussar born in faraway lands. Court clerks were drawing up all kinds of public documents on paper that had been issued in the reign of Don Fernando VII, and to which was being added the following note: "Valid for the reign of King José Napoleón I." And all those sons of Voltaire and Rousseau condescended to hear Mass on Sundays and holy days, even though generals and other superior officers heard it, as befitted their high station, lounging in the armchairs of the chancel and smoking enormous pipes. The monks of San Agustín, San Diego, Santo Domingo, and San Francisco had "consumed" all the consecrated hosts and evacuated, under orders, their monasteries so that the French could convert them into barracks. In short, all was enforced peace, official joy, and enthusiasm on penalty of death in the former court of those other enemies of Christ who reigned in Guadix by the grace of Allah and his prophet Mahomet.

II

It was under these circumstances that the slaughterhouse of Guadix had to close its doors for want of animals to kill. Cows, oxen, calves, sheep, goats—all the livestock in the territory had been devoured by those foreigners, in addition to all the hams, shoulders, turkeys, chickens, hens, pigeons, and tame city rabbits, because never had human beings been seen continually eating so much meat.

The locals, always frugal as a result of being half-African, continued eating raw, boiled or fried vegetables, but the Conqueror needed meat, and fresh meat, and plenty of it, and right away.

In the midst of this predicament the French general remembered that the territory of Guadix consisted of a number of towns, and that the majority of them were yet to be conquered.

"It's necessary," he then said to his troops, "for the eagle of the Empire to be known far and wide. Spread out through all the towns, villages, and farms in the territory under my command; take them the good news of the accession of Don José I to the throne of San

Fernando; take possession of them in his name and bring me upon your return all the livestock that you find in their corrals and sheepfolds. Long live the emperor!"

And in consequence of this order of the day, ten or twelve columns, each one made up of one hundred to two hundred men, left in the direction of the marquisate of Zenet, Gor, the hill country, and the towns situated on the northern slope of the Sierra Nevada range.

Among the latter—and now we've come to the episode to which I referred when I picked up my pen today—among the towns which, indifferent to the advances of civilization, are stagnating at the foot of the colossal and perpetually snowcapped Mulhacén peak,* lies one that was and still is renowned sixty miles around for the indomitable character of its inhabitants, their fierce appearance, the near savage state of their customs, and other peculiarities which will emerge in this account. I refer to the very old town of Lapeza, famous during the war against the Moors, and whose ruinous old castle still recalls the name of its brave governor, Bernardino de Villalta, a worthy adversary of the followers of Abén-Humeya.*

It was the 15th of April in the above-mentioned year of 1810.

The small town of Lapeza presented an unusual sight—as ludicrous as it was admirable, as grotesque as it was impressive, and as ridiculous as it was frightening. All of its streets were barricaded with a wall of oak trunks and other gigantic trees which the townspeople en masse brought down from the nearby mountain and with which they built piles not easily scaled. As the great majority of that community is made up of charcoal burners, and the rest of woodcutters and shepherds, the operation just described was carried out with a truly astonishing speed and efficiency.

The sturdy wooden wall formed a kind of tower alongside the road to Guadix, and on top of this tower the people of Lapeza had positioned—if you can imagine it!—a huge cannon which they themselves had constructed, a cannon that has gone down in history. It was fashioned from an enormous oak trunk, hollowed out by fire, and wrapped with strong rope and extra thick wire, loaded to the muzzle with ample powder and packed with shot, stone, pieces of spent iron, and other similar projectiles.

They had collected in addition all manner of arms from the town and mountain, which resulted in a dozen or so shotguns, more than twenty blunderbusses and muskets, a knife, dagger, or razor per person, three or four dozen woodcutting axes, several flintlock pistols, huge piles of sizable stones with all the slings needed to hurl them, and a veritable forest of assorted clubs and cudgels.

As for the "garrison," all those who witnessed the episode agree that it consisted of around two hundred "men," and they could be called such only by an excess of generosity, as they looked more like orangutans than men. Among those on the front line, one who deserves special mention and one who will give an exact idea of the others, was the general of that army, the governor of that stronghold, the mayor of Lapeza, Manuel Atienza. God rest his soul!

This high official was a man between forty-five and fifty, as tall as a cypress, as big-boned or gnarled (which is more apt) as an ash, and as strong as an oak, although to tell the truth, his many years as a charcoal burner had blackened him to such a degree that if he did resemble an oak it was an oak turned into charcoal. His fingernails looked like flint, his teeth like mahogany, and his hands like sun-deepened bronze; his hair, because it was disheveled and littered with straw, looked like uncrushed hemp, while because of the color and appearance it looked like the back of a wild boar; his chest, exposed by an unbuttoned shirt from shoulder to shoulder and from the neck down to the belly, seemed to be covered with a horsehide that had wrinkled and hardened from working around live coals, and indeed the bristly hair that blanketed his prominent breastbone was singed, as were his bushy eyebrows. And this was due to the fact that His Honor the mayor was a charcoal burner (that is, "a mountain cook," as they style themselves), and had spent all his life in the middle of a fire, like the souls in purgatory.

With regard to Manuel Atienza's eyes, no one could deny that they "saw," but no one would ever have claimed that they "looked." His Honor's recognized ignorance, together with a simian slyness and the cautiousness of a man advanced in years, restrained him from ever fixing his gaze on his interlocutors lest they discover gaps in his intelligence or knowledge. And if he did fix it, he did so in such an indolent, suspicious, and furtive fashion that it seemed as though those pupils were peering inward or that he had two more eyes behind his ears like lizards. Finally, his mouth looked like an old mastiff's; his forehead disappeared with the progression of hair; his face shone like tanned leather; and his voice, hoarse like a shot from a blunderbuss, had a sharp, rasping sound like ax blows on firewood.

Needless to say, his dress, which was what the well-off in those towns wore, consisted of bull's hide sandals and a burner's apron;

woolen stockings; short breeches and a jacket of the same dark, coarse cloth; a sky-blue satin vest with a yellow floral pattern; a leather cartridge belt instead of a sash; and an enormous hat underneath whose brim, trimmed with plush, rested very comfortably all his authority.

And speaking of authority, I'll add by way of conclusion that the mayor's wand of office reached his shoulder, and that his two black tassels, as big as two oranges, proclaimed far and wide a "man of law and order," as we would say nowadays.

Such was the mayor of Lapeza, and all his subordinates were cut from the same mold. If you think the description is exaggerated, bear in mind that the race of Lapezians has neither degenerated nor been modified with the passage of years. Go there, and you'll be astonished, as I was, that in Spain, and in the middle of the 19th century, exist all the wonders of northern Africa.*

III

But the work of fortification was completed and the arms had been distributed all around.

Atienza had sent Jacinto to his house for an ancient drum that was used in processions, at bullfights, and to announce proclamations.

Jacinto—who, by the way, was the bailiff and died in office in the current year of 1859—returned sounding the call to arms.

"Fall in!" shouted the magistrate, well-versed in the art of warfare, inasmuch as he had served King Carlos IV as a mess cook in a company of chasseurs.

The two hundred Lapezians took their arms and lined up in battle order opposite the town hall.

Atienza then grasped a large and very old black sword with a wide guard and a long quillon; he shoved a saddle pistol into his cartridge belt; he took the mayoral wand in his left hand, just as a marshal of France would take his baton, and, followed by a brilliant staff made up of the bailiff, the town crier or "public servant," and the "Undersigned," which is what, by antonomasia, the notary's wife called her husband, he reviewed his formidable army, which presented arms or tossed their caps and hats in the air.

"Long live the mayor!" shouted or barked those future heroes.

To which Atienza retorted:

"Mayor, my foot! Long live God! Long live Lapeza! Long live Spanish independence!"

After this martial exchange, His Honor ordered Jacinto to play a long drumroll and summoned the town crier, who repeated one by one, and almost syllable by syllable, the words of their leader's unwritten proclamation:

"From news—brought by—old Piorno—it's been learned—that our country's enemy—is coming to—Lapeza today—to set upon us—and steal our property; and we—with our priest's blessing—and the help—of our patron saint—the Virgin of the Rosary—are going—to defend ourselves—like good Spaniards—and show—the town of Guadix—that if it—has surrendered—to the French—the people of Lapeza—know how to die—as did—the people of Madrid—on the 2nd of May—or triumph—as did—the people of Bailén—two years ago—and consequently—the mayor informs—the men here gathered—that whoever—does not die—this day—in defense—of his homeland—will be declared—a despicable Spaniard—a traitor—to his country—and will die—as is fitting—hanged from—a mountain oak.—And let—the record show—that His Honor—not knowing—how to sign—makes his usual cross—for which—the notary vouches.—Long live God!—Long live the Virgin!—Long live Spain!—Long live Fernando VII!—Death to Pepe Botellas!*—Death to the French!—Death to Godinot!—Death to the traitors!"

This combination martial proclamation and legal proceeding produced an extraordinary effect on the Lapezians.

Manuel Atienza made the cross with his fingers and kissed it at the mention of the signature; the notary vouched with a nod of the head; the town crier congratulated the mayor on how well he had improvised his speech; Jacinto played another drumroll; and the *Vivas*, dances, and patriotic hymns ended that comic "prologue" to a genuine tragedy.

"Each one to his post!" the magistrate then exclaimed.

And some of them scaled the wooden fortress; others, holding a long fuse, mounted the cannon; the peasants most accomplished with a sling climbed the Moorish citadel; the musketeers left to scout the road to Guadix; and the mayor positioned himself at a vantage point that commanded the future battlefield, with Jacinto at his side, so that with a drumroll he could signal "commence fire."

Meanwhile, the priest was once again blessing and absolving his brave parishioners, and, along with the veterinarian, the sacristan, and the gravedigger, devoted himself to preparing bandages, Holy Oil, and stretchers to minister to the wounded and dead.

Almost all the women were praying in the church; and as for the children, it had been decided that morning to send all of them to the top of the Sierra Nevada so that their lives would not be in danger and that they could, in years to come, serve to repel another foreign invasion.

IV

It was approximately three o'clock in the afternoon when a cloud of dust warned the Lapezians of the proximity of the enemy.

Several shots fired a moment later by an advance party confirmed the warning.

The Lapezians jumped with excitement and, at the same time, executed the mayor's last order by hoisting two or three flags made of black handkerchiefs on the old Moorish citadel and the oak barricade.

Bells sounded the alarm; many old women began to scream and boys started to whistle; some stones whizzed through the air; and the gunshots from the road to Guadix were closer and more frequent.

Shortly afterwards the musketeers withdrew toward the town, reloading their weapons, and the first helmets, cuirasses, and bayonets of the invading army glanced within range of the muskets and blunderbusses.

"How many are there?" Manuel Atienza asked one of the musketeers who had scouted furthest ahead.

"Around two hundred," the latter replied.

"We're equal forces!" the charcoal burner exclaimed with disdainful arrogance, disregarding the fact that two hundred poorly armed peasants were no match for two hundred battle-hardened veterans attacking with the best in armament.

"But they have cavalry!" added a second musketeer.

"I repeat: we're equal forces!" Manuel Atienza said. "All right, Jacinto, let's hear that drum! And let's fight for Spain! Long live the Virgin!"

Jacinto gave the anxiously awaited signal and a shower of stones and shot fell on the Frenchmen and forced them to halt.

Shortly afterwards they replied with a heavy volley, wounding five Lapezians.

"Cease fire!" the mayor then shouted. "They're still too far away and we don't have that much powder. Let's let them get closer. You know that we're saving the cannon for the last moment, and that until I fling my hat nobody puts the fuse to it. And you, ladies, I wonder if you can quiet down and attend to the wounded."

"Here they come again!"

"Easy. Everybody keep still!"

"They're aiming!"

"Everybody down!"

A second volley smashed into the oak logs, and the French advanced to within twenty paces of the besieged Lapezians.

The infantrymen fell back on both sides of the road, allowing the cavalry to pass.

"Fire!" the mayor then shouted in a stentorian voice as he tossed his hat in the air and braved extreme danger.

What happened next was horrible beyond words.

Frenchmen and Spaniards fired their weapons at the same time, strewing the ground with corpses, and the cavalry took advantage of the moment to gallop toward the foot of the wooden barricade, thinking, undoubtedly, that they could storm it with their powerful steeds. Hundreds of stones knocked down both horses and riders, and the latter began to swing their sabers with impunity; and in that absolute turmoil, in the midst of that whirlwind and destruction and confusion the awesome cannon shot finally erupted, producing an ear-splitting explosion and raining death on besieged and besiegers.

And it was because the "cannon" had exploded upon firing; it was because the oak trunk, blown into smithereens, discharged shot in every direction—forward, backward, and both sides—shot mixed with a thousand wood fragments that whistled as they swished through the air; it was because the explosion of so much ignited powder had made the logs on which the cannon rested begin to roll, and these logs crushed Spaniards and Frenchmen alike. The scene was a chaos of smoke, powder, screams, moans, whinnying, flames, and blood; of mutilated corpses whose limbs were still flying through the air or falling back to earth amid shot, stones, and other projectiles; of Lapezians who were still on their feet striking blind blows at friend and foe; of dagger thrusts, pistol shots, and thrown stones that came from below, from above, from everywhere, as if the world had come to an end.

And in the middle of this tempest, this inferno, one heard simultaneously the French bugle sounding retreat and the Lapezian drumroll beating the call to arms, while the voice of the redoubtable charcoal burner, the invincible mayor, the invulnerable Atienza rose above the din as he shouted furiously:

"Don't let up, boys! Get every last one! There can't be many left now!"

And it was true, but it was also true that there were even fewer Spaniards left. The oak cannon had wreaked more havoc among the Lapezians than the Frenchmen.

Nevertheless, as the latter knew neither the means of defense that the Spanish devils could have had in reserve nor their number, and as they were now in dread of them, they thought only of saving themselves as quickly as possible; and, scattered and dispersed, with the cavalry trampling the infantry and soldiers ignoring their officers' orders, the Frenchmen began a retreat very similar to a flight, pursued by peasants who had a plentiful supply of stones for their slings and musketeers who still had ammunition.

Having been stoned, shot at, blackened by powder and covered with sweat and dust, and having left one hundred men in Lapeza and on the road, the conquerors of Egypt, Italy, and Germany entered Guadix at eight o'clock in the evening, defeated that day by an "inferior force" of shepherds and charcoal burners.

V

The bloody drama that we've just related could not help having a terrible epilogue. Our readers can imagine the surprise and rage of General Godinot when he learned what had happened in Lapeza.

"I shall reduce it to rubble!" exclaimed the vengeful Frenchman.

And four days later there left for the town governed by Atienza twenty-four hundred heavily armed troops under the command of a general officer, and with sufficient supplies and munitions to lay siege to a fortress.

That large army came within sight of Lapeza at nine o'clock in the morning.

They didn't encounter a soul on the road, didn't hear a shot, didn't ward off a single stone. It was all silence and solitude in the bloodied town.

The demolished log wall had not been repaired, nor did the bells warn of the enemy's arrival.

Thus did the angry invaders enter the town.

And a kind of foreshadowing must have crossed their minds, an inkling of what happened to them in Russia. Lapeza was deserted, just like Moscow when Napoleon the Great set foot in it.

The wolves, satiated with carnage, had disappeared again into the interior of the sierra.

Only a few poor women, who had come down that day to rummage their abandoned homes for food to take back, were found in the corners of the church where they had sought refuge, believing that the illustrious conquerors would not violate them there.

But . . . no! In the absence of strong men to overcome, perfidious fortune offered them hapless maidens to affront, innocence to mock, and virtue to sully with ignominy and bitterness.

Let us turn away from these infamous deeds, repeated over and over by the conquerors of Europe during their odious rule in Spain. A curse and shame on those who take advantage of victory to commit crimes! Everlasting horror of foreign arms!

Elated and satisfied, the French heroes were returning along the road to Guadix with but two prisoners in tow from that loud expedition—an unarmed, decrepit, and infirm old man whom they found in a shack and a timid youth who was taking care of him—when news of what had happened in their homes was spread throughout the sierra by one of the aggrieved women, which precipitated an attack by enraged fathers, brothers, and fiancés who dashed down the mountain like rushing streams.

There then began a tremendous flying battle (the graphic description) between the one hundred men still under the orders of Atienza and the French expeditionary force of twenty-four hundred soldiers.

After throwing down the gauntlet and initiating the action, the Lapezians began to retreat, in Moorish fashion, with the aim of drawing their enemy into the dense interior of the sierra.

The Frenchmen carelessly fell into the trap, and although it is true that their terrible arms nearly wiped out that handful of brave men, it is likewise true that they paid for each life with ten casualties from their own ranks.

The rugged rocks, green ravines, thickets, and defiles were strewn with French corpses.

It was one of many little-known losses suffered in Spain by the Napoleonic forces, losses which did not figure in the bulletins of the great battles, but which at the end of the War of Independence added up to the staggering sum of half a million imperial soldiers lost or killed in our peninsula.

Let us finish.

Atienza—or "Atencia," which was how His Honor pronounced his name—the unbeaten charcoal burner who had taken the fight to Bonaparte's troops twice in four days, was standing atop a very high cliff, surrounded by Frenchmen; cornered, trapped, loading his blunderbuss with the last cartridge; his head bandaged as a result of the battle fought on the 15th; recently wounded in the chest and all covered with blood; the wand of his office inside his belt after the manner of a muleteer, he was responding to calls that he give himself up with savage guffaws that echoed through the mountain canyons.

Countless bullets whistled around him continually, but he dodged them, jumping from side to side, springing into the air, and ducking; agile, quick, and nimble, like a tiger constantly on the move, he crouched, leaped, turned up everywhere, and struck fear whether defending or attacking.

He fired, finally, the last round in his blunderbuss, arcing the terrible weapon as if he wanted to spray the mountain with shot. At that very moment a bullet hit him in the abdomen and he let out a terrifying howl. Knowing that he was going to die, he hurled his now useless blunderbuss, not without first looking at it angrily, removed the long wand from his belt, and said to a French colonel who was urging him in bad Spanish to give himself up:

"I will not surrender!" he yelled. "I am the town of Lapeza, and I will die before I surrender!"

And breaking the staff of his office with his hands, he threw the pieces into the Frenchmen's faces and jumped backward, smashing against the crags of a deep ravine, the fall cracking and shattering his strong bones.

The enemy did not even manage to capture him dead!

VI

Lapeza was now in French hands.

General Godinot heard the news from the commander of the expeditionary force.

"How many prisoners have you taken?" the former asked the latter. "We need to hang them to teach a lesson to the other towns in the district."

"Only two: an old man and a boy. I didn't find anyone else in the whole town!" the commander replied with downcast eyes.

Godinot could not help admiring the old and truly classic, Spartan attitude of those mountain people. But, even so, he insisted that the two frail prisoners be hanged.

Our parents have related to us many times the details of that execution.

But we'll give a quick account of it as the former are of too ferocious a nature to dwell upon them.

They tied a rope around the boy's neck and hanged him from a balcony of the town hall that gave onto the main square of Guadix.

The rope snapped and the boy fell to the stone pavement.

They knotted the two ends, raised the poor creature again, hanged him another time, and the rope snapped once more.

The boy lay on the pavement unable to move. He hadn't died, but all his limbs were broken.

Then, seeing that they were going to hang him a third time, a dragoon officer approached the wretched youth and finished him off with a pistol shot to the head.

With their ferocity appeased in such a manner, at least for that day, the conquerors deigned to spare the life of the infirm old man, who had witnessed all of the above scene curled up at the foot of a pillar, waiting for his turn to be hanged.

So they set him free, and the miserable thing, staggering and reeling, fled from the square and took the road home, where he died that very night from sorrow.

The boy murdered in Guadix was his son.

GUADIX, 1859

El ángel de la guarda

The Guardian Angel

I

"**MARTINS** come back on May 1st," has been said in Spain from time immemorial to express the fact that every year, to the day, martins and swifts, after their winter journey to Africa, return to our land, or rather, to our skies. But what nobody has said until now, and what I have on very good authority, is that martins have probably never sighted the walls of Tarragona anew, nor taken possession there of old nests, on a more beautiful, radiant, and fragrant day than May 1st, 1814.

The sea, as blue and calm as the sky itself, looked, not like an extension of finite land, but like the beginning of eternity and infinity. The countryside received the sun's caresses with a smile, and repaid them with colorful flowers, the harbinger and assurance of delicious fruits. The atmosphere, in short, was impregnated with love and life, and in its tepid gusts one could detect the scented breath of spring, already enamored of summer.

But the spring charms of that unforgettable day were not solely of this kind. People in cities, when thinking about the return of the migratory birds, and that the month of flowers had begun, and that the following day would be the second of May, experienced solemn and agreeable sensations—moral, patriotic feelings that also spoke to their spirit of resurrection and renewal. Barely a fortnight had passed since peace reigned in Spain, after six years of incessant fighting! The *War of Independence*, the epic of which our parents were the heroes and heroines, was all over. Napoleon's generals had fled with their armies and with their supposed king to tell the conqueror of so many nations that it was folly to think about subjugating the Spanish people. There was no longer a single foreign soldier in the entire peninsula.

So our impoverished and debilitated homeland was resting in the light of that resplendent sun, like a convalescent who leaves his bed after fighting continually against death. A melancholy and sublime time! Once more bells summoned the faithful to burned out, sacked churches; once more smoke from bloodstained fireplaces rose through the serene atmosphere; and once more popular old songs were sung. Valiant patriots laid down their arms and returned to their labors, consoling themselves at having lost sons, brothers, and fathers with one thought: they had saved the land where their loved ones had been born and died. There was, in short, nothing but sacred sadness and pathetic joy, from San Sebastián to Cádiz, from La Coruña to Gerona; nothing but tales of glorious deeds from one province to another, from one city to another, from one village to another, all of which had acted in concert to throw off the foreign yoke; nothing but giving thanks to God for the victory, remembering the deceased in prayer, and restoring or rebuilding cities with the hope of living a longer and more fruitful life in them than the heroic martyrs of the homeland.

II

On the morning in question, a gallant young man and a stunning young woman, dressed simply and in good taste, like well-off members of the middle class, were leaving Santo Domingo church in Tarragona, where they had just kept an all-night vigil.

The same priest who had married them the week before now amicably accompanied the loving couple, walking very pleased and proud between them as if they owed him all their happiness.

They did owe him a great deal. Manuel and Clara, the names of the young people, had each lost their families on June 28, 1811, when General Suchet took Tarragona by storm. Two years later, at the conclusion of the campaign of 1813, Suchet, on the run, passed through the same city and blew up its fortresses and some houses, one of the latter being that of the court clerk who held all the deeds to properties owned by Manuel, at the time a fugitive, along with Clara and her mother. On those two dreadful occasions more than half of the inhabitants of Tarragona had perished, so that when Manuel returned as a hapless orphan in search of his house and his possessions to offer them to those two destitute women, he found that it wasn't possible to establish his identity, much less prove his right to his parents' estate. It was at this juncture that the virtuous priest in whose company we now find him showed up in the pillaged city. He had known Manuel since birth (because he had always been the parish priest and had baptized him and taught him to read), and as a consequence of the sworn statement made by this elderly minister of the Lord, Manuel—who was already begging!—became rich the very next day.

Not many weeks afterward he married Clara.

As for the latter's mother, she'll appear in the course of our short and true tale.

III

"**So**, my children, tell me. What's this all about?" the priest asked at the door to the church.

"It's about the fact, Father," Clara said sadly, "that we have a secret to confide to you."

"A secret? To me? Didn't I hear your confessions this morning?"

"Yes, Father," Manuel answered even more sadly, "but our secret isn't a sin."

"Well, then, that's another matter!"

"At least it's not *our* sin," interjected the newly-wed wife.

"I knew there had to be something wrong when you sought out these weary old bones. All right now. What's going on?"

"You tell him," Clara said to her husband.

Manuel only said the following:

"Not here. Come with us. It's a lovely morning. We'll take a short stroll, and *at the very site* we'll tell you what's going on."

"At what site?"

"Not here. Come with us," Clara repeated, tugging at the priest's cloak.

The cleric willingly acceded to the young couple's request and they began to walk. About a half mile beyond the city limits, and on the very bank of the Francolí River, Manuel stopped, saying:

"It was here."

"No, no," Clara corrected him. "It was further on."

"You're right. It was at that bend, where there's a woman sitting on the ground."

"Well, I'll be! That woman's my mother!"

"What? Your mother?"

"It is. I'm certain. She left the house this morning, as she does every day, without letting anybody accompany her. And look where the poor thing goes! Don't be surprised, Father; you know that the miserable woman isn't in her right mind. Ever since *that night* she suffers frequent lapses of reason."

At this point the priest, Manuel, and Clara arrived at the side of a woman who was in fact sitting on the ground, at the edge of the water, staring at the swift current of the Francolí.

She was an elderly woman of venerable demeanor, with a severe and wizened face, pitch-black eyes, and a head of thick white hair; a Catalan mother, in a word, as energetic as she was gentle, as affectionate as she was proud.

"What a beautiful day, Mother!" Clara said to distract her as she embraced her.

"What a horrible night, my child!" the poor madwoman replied.

"You'll see how it all happened, Father," Manuel said, making an effort and moving the priest away from the two women.

IV

"There lies, Father," Manuel began, pointing to the river, "in those currents that have washed away so much blood for five years, a martyr of Spanish independence, a baby boy who died fifteen months after his birth, and to whom, nevertheless, these two hearts that you have united forever owe their life and happiness. I won't speak of Clara's mother, because even though she also owes her life to that blessed child, she would've been better off dying with him. You see what a state the miserable thing is in.

"You're amazed, Father, that an innocent infant can do so much good for his family at the age of fifteen months. I understand. Not only am I amazed too, I'm dying of shame. But you're aware of what happened to me that night."

As he said this, Manuel showed the parish priest his left hand, horribly disfigured by a long, deep scar.

"At fifteen months, yes! He died at the age of fifteen months, and his life wasn't useless, it wasn't in vain. Many people live a long time without doing so much good for their fellow man. God has him, beyond a shadow of a doubt, not in the company of angels, but with martyrs and heroes.

"You already know what a sorrowful day June 28, 1811, was for

Tarragona. However, having been taken prisoner during the attack on May 4th you didn't see all the horror of the city's capture. You didn't see five thousand Spaniards die in ten hours; you didn't see houses and churches set on fire; you didn't see defenseless old men and frail women murdered; you didn't see the trampling of virgins' virtue, mothers' dignity, nuns' chastity. You didn't see plunder and drunkenness mixed with lust and slaughter. You didn't see, in short, one of the greatest exploits of the conqueror of the world, of the hero of our times, of the semigod Napoleon.

"I saw it all. I saw the ill leave their deathbeds, dragging their sheets like a shroud, and perish at the hands of foreign soldiers on the threshold of the very bedroom where the viaticum had entered the day before. I saw, lying down on this road, a woman with her throat slit, and at her side a young baby, still sucking at his dead mother's breast. I saw handcuffed husbands witness the desecration of the marriage bed and children who cried in the midst of so much horror; I saw the desperate and innocent resort to suicide, and the impious jeer at corpses. Oh! Damn foreign arms!

"My father and brothers died on that day of agonizing memory. Lucky them!

"As I was very seriously wounded and unable to fight, I sought refuge in Clara's house.

"Overcome with anguish and dread, she was waiting at the balcony, afraid for my life and risking hers to see me if I happened along the street.

"I went in, but my pursuers saw her . . . and she was so beautiful!

"A beauty who was greeted by a roar of savage joy and a brutal peal of laughter. A minute later axes and flames were gutting our door. We were done for.

"Clara's mother, carrying in her arms the unfortunate child who lies under those currents, shut herself up with us in the house's cistern or reservoir, which was very deep, as well as dry, because it hadn't rained in many months. That cistern, whose surface measured perhaps eight square yards, and which was reached by descending long subterranean ramps, narrowed at the top, like the mouth of a well, and rose in the middle of the patio where the curb stood; a pulley hung from an iron hoop to permit water to be drawn by means of two small pails.

"The baby boy, named Miguel, was Clara's brother, in other words, the youngest child of the miserable woman whom the French had just left a widow.

"Inside the cistern the four of us could escape, or rather, we had already escaped. It wouldn't have occurred to anybody that we were down there, nor that such a place existed! From above, the cistern looked like an ordinary well. The French would believe that we had fled along the roof of the house.

"They soon expressed that very idea, amidst horrifying oaths, while they rested in the cool patio, in the middle of which was the cistern.

"Yes, we had escaped! Clara was bandaging my wound; her mother was nursing Miguel; and I, although shivering from the chill of a fever, was smiling happily.

"At this point we realized that the French, dying of thirst, were trying to draw water from the cistern that hid us.

"Imagine our terror at that instant.

"We stood aside and let the pail be lowered until it hit the ground.

"We didn't even breathe.

"The pail was raised again.

"'It's dry!' said the Frenchmen.

"'We'll find water further up!' one of them exclaimed.

"They're leaving! Clara, her mother, and I thought.

"'What if they're hiding inside?' asked a voice in Catalan.

"It was a *French sympathizer,* Father! It was a Spaniard who was betraying us!

"'How absurd,' answered the Frenchmen. 'They wouldn't have been able to descend so quickly.'

"'I guess you're right," agreed the French sympathizer.

"They didn't know that you went down to the cistern through the shaft, whose door or trapdoor, well concealed on the floor of a somewhat distant and dark wine cellar, was very difficult to spot. On the other hand, we had been imprudent enough to lock the iron gate that blocked passage between the cistern and shaft, and we couldn't open it without making a lot of noise.

"Imagine, if you will, the cruel fluctuation between hope and fear with which we listened to the dialogue carried on by those devils at the very curb of the well. From the corner where we were crouching, we saw the shadows of their heads move in the circle of light that shone from above on the bottom of the dry cistern. Every second seemed like a century to us.

"At this point Miguel started to cry.

"But no sooner had he let out his first howl than his mother smothered the voice that was giving us away, squeezing the infant's face against her breast.

"'Did you hear that?' they shouted above.

"'I didn't,' another answered.

"'Let's listen,' said the French sympathizer.

"Three horrible minutes went by.

"Miguel was struggling to cry, and the more his mother smothered him, the more furious he got and the more he writhed in her arms.

"But not even the slightest sigh was heard.

"'It must have been an echo,' exclaimed the Frenchmen as they moved away.

"'That must be it,' the French sympathizer added.

"They all left, and the noise of their footsteps and sabers slowly died out as they walked along the patio in the direction of the street gate.

"The danger had passed.

"But, oh . . . our happiness was short-lived.

"Miguel wasn't crying or struggling now.

"He was dead!"

V

"Father! Father!" Clara's mother shouted at this point, interrupting Manuel. "Say that it's a lie. I didn't kill my son. *They* killed him. I smothered him to save *them*. He suffocated to save all of us. Oh, Father, forgive me. I'm not a bad woman. I've lost my mind because of my Miguel, because of my precious son. I'm not a bad mother."

"Father," Clara said. "We've brought you to this spot to bless the water where we threw the corpse of my brother when we fled Tarragona the night of June 28, 1811. The danger that we were in didn't give us time to bury him."

"Isn't it true that Miguel's in heaven, Father?" Manuel asked, wiping away his tears.

"Yes, my children," replied the priest. "I assure you that he is, in the name of God and in the name of our homeland. And you, don't cry," he continued, speaking to the elderly woman. "God blesses the martyrdom that you're undergoing, as I bless the innocent child who caused it. You'll find your son in heaven, and with him joy of the soul." And turning to Manuel and Clara, he said: "As for you, who can be so happy in this life, don't forget that you bought your happiness at the cost of the suffering of others. So you suffer too when your fellow man needs you."

Thus spoke the priest, and, in the light of the spring sun, in the middle of the flowery countryside, to the sound of birds' music, accompanied in short, by all the joys of Nature, he blessed the place where the waters of the Francolí served as a grave for the fortunate child who was his family's "Guardian Angel."

MADRID, 1859

Notes

Page references to this volume precede each note.

(27) *Larra, Kock, Soulié:* Mariano José de Larra (1809–1837), Spanish satirist and author of articles on customs and politics; Charles Paul de Kock (1793–1871), French novelist and playwright; Frédéric Soulié (1800–1847), French novelist and playwright.

(29) *Puerta del Sol:* central commercial square in nineteenth-century Madrid.

(30) *Kamchatka Peninsula:* in northeastern Siberia; it separates the Sea of Okhotsk in the west from the Bering Sea and the Pacific Ocean in the east.

(30) *Gertrudis . . . thunderbolt:* Gertrudis Gómez de Avellaneda (1816–1873), Cuban poet, novelist, and playwright who settled in Spain. She gained renown for her historical plays, one of which is *Alfonso Munio.*

(44) *Holding . . . everything:* the myth of Ariadne, daughter of Minos and Pasiphaë, who gave Theseus the thread by which he escaped from the labyrinth.

(48) *Mirabeau:* Honoré Gabriel Mirabeau (1749–1791), French Revolutionary leader famous for his oratory.

(62) *Baldomero Espartero* (1793–1879): liberal general who supported Queen Isabel and fought against the pretender Don Carlos.

(63) *Mazzepa . . . hero:* in Canto IV of the poem *Mazzepa* (1819).

(63) *Carlos and Isabel:* The Carlist Wars. The Salic Law introduced in Spain in 1713 by Felipe V of the Bourbon line excluded females from the throne. Although it was abrogated as the Pragmatic Sanction by the Cortes [Parliament] in 1789 at the request of Carlos IV, the change was never published nor printed in the collection of laws. The tryannical Fernando VII, eldest son of Carlos IV, was childless after the death of his first three wives; he married his fourth, María Cristina, 12 December 1829. Several months later, in March of 1830, he decreed the royal Pragmatic Sanction so that Cristina's children, even if female, could succeed to the throne. After his death on 29 September 1833, his brother Carlos (to become known as the Pretender) contested Fernando's will, which provided for Cristina to rule as regent for their two-year-old daughter Isabel. The civil wars that ensued bore his name; the first Carlist War was from 1833–40, the second from 1846–48, and the third (and last) from 1872–76.

(64) *Navarre:* north central Spain, bordering on France.

(65) *Alava:* province in northern Spain, the Basque country.

(72) *Duke . . . Portugal:* Duke of Reichstadt, Napoleon II (1811–1832), son of

Napoleon I and Marie Louise; Louis XVII (1785–1795), titular boy king of France who died in prison; Pope Joan, fictitious being, from the Spanish *papisa,* or "woman pope"; Prester John, a legendary priest and king of the Middle Ages reputed to have had a kingdom in the Far East; Sebastian (1554–1578), king of Portugal, whose unreported death at the Battle (1578) of Al Qasr al Kabir (Morocco) gave rise to the legend that he would return.

(73) *Totana:* city in the province of Murcia, southeastern Spain.

(75) *Gironella:* in Catalonia, north-northwest of Barcelona.

(78) *Orderlies . . . then:* orderlies, in this context, would seem to imply a number of them. Alarcón has apparently forgotten that the captain stated that he has had but two.

(79) *Don . . . Panza: Don Quijote,* II, 42.

(79) *War of Independence:* 1808–1814. The war fought by Spaniards, aided by English troops under Wellington, against the Napoleonic invasion and the installation of Joseph Bonaparte on the throne of Spain.

(81) *Not . . . 1823:* During the War of Independence Spanish liberals rejected absolutism and drew up a new liberal constitution at Cádiz in 1812. When Ferdinand VII was restored to the Spanish throne he refused to honor the 1812 constitution and reinstated the privileges of nobility and clergy, which precipitated the revolution of 1820. It was this revolution which was suppressed by French troops in 1823 in the name of the Holy Alliance.

(82) *Didón:* In all likelihood a Spanish corruption of the French *Dis, donc* (Look here). Used as a disparaging term.

(85) *Risas:* Literally, (peals of) laughter.

(88) *Descendant . . . fist:* Diego García de Paredes (1466–1520), Spanish army officer renowned for his strength.

(90) *May 2nd in Madrid:* in 1808, date of the uprising by the people of Madrid, brutally repressed by French troops, which marked the beginning of the War of Independence. Benito Pérez Galdós gives an account of it in his *The 19th of March and the 2nd of May,* one of his "National Episodes" (novels based on historical events and personages), and it is also the subject of a painting by Francisco de Goya in Madrid's Prado Museum.

(90) *Battle . . . Pyramids:* the name given by Napoleon to his victorious battle against the Mamelukes fought near Embaba, July 1798.

(90) *Milo:* Greek Olympic athlete born in Crotona (Italy), as celebrated for his strength as the biblical Samson (*Judges,* 13–16). Other references in this paragraph: Granada was the last Moorish kingdom to be taken (in 1492) in the Reconquest carried out by the Catholic monarchs, King Ferdinand of Aragón and Queen Isabella of Castile; the Quirinal is one of the seven hills of Rome and site of a papal palace constructed in the 16th century; Alejandro Borja [Borgia], a Spaniard, was pope (1492–1503) as Alexander VI; in the famous battle of Pavia (which is south of Milan) the Spaniards defeated the French in 1525 and Charles V captured Francis I, king of France; and Joaquim Murat (1767–1815), Napoleon's brother-in-law and one of his most brilliant commanders, was king of Naples from 1808

to 1815.

(96) *Like . . . ones:* Alarcón is referring to the two War of Independence stories that precede this one and the two that follow it.

(97) *Gerona:* city in northwestern Catalonia, immortalized in the War of Independence when the French laid siege to it. *Gerona* is another of Pérez Galdós's "National Episodes."

(101) *Consummatum est:* It is done (i.e., the French takeover).

(106) *The . . . Lapeza:* The literal translation of "El carbonero alcalde" is "The Charcoal Burner Mayor." The burners of Lapeza called themselves "mountain cooks" because the old method of making [wood] charcoal consisted of piling wood into stacks, covering it with earth, and "burning" it until the resulting carbon was converted into charcoal. The proximity of fire made the work hot, dirty, and sometimes dangerous for the burners.

(108) *Mulhacén peak:* in Granada's Sierra Nevada; at 11,410 feet it is the highest peak in the Iberian peninsula.

(108) *Abén-Humeya* (1520–1568): leader of the Moorish rebellion against Philip II.

(110) *northern Africa:* Although Alarcón writes *Africa meridional* or *southern Africa,* "northern [Africa]" would make more sense in context as the Moors of Andalusia traced their ancesters to the peoples of ancient Mauretania [NW Africa] who invaded Spain in the eighth century.

(111) *Pepe Botellas:* "Joe Bottles," the name Spaniards gave to Napoleon's brother whom they considered, mistakenly, an alcoholic.

Select Bibliography

First Editions of Alarcón's Short Stories

El clavo (causa célebre). Granada: M. de Benavides, 1854.

Cuentos, artículos y novelas. Series 1ª, 2ª, y 3ª. Madrid: Imprenta de El Atalaya, 1859.

Novelas. Madrid: Durán, 1866.

Cosas que fueron. Madrid: Imprenta de La Correspondencia de España, 1871.

Amores y amoríos: historietas en prosa y verso. Madrid: A. de Carlos e hijos editores, 1875.

Novelas cortas, 1ª serie: Cuentos amatorios. Madrid: Imprenta y fundición de Tello, 1881. (Prepared by the author.)

Novelas cortas, 2ª serie: Historietas nacionales. Madrid: Imprenta y fundición de Tello, 1881. (Prepared by the author.)

Novelas cortas, 3ª serie: Narraciones inverosímiles. Madrid: Imprenta y fundición de Tello, 1882. (Prepared by the author.)

Twentieth-Century Collections of the Short Stories

Dos ángeles caídos y otros escritos olvidados. Ed. Agustín Aguilar y Tejera. Madrid: Imprenta Latina, 1924.

Cuentos amatorios. Madrid: Librería General de Victoriano Suárez, 1943. Contains all the stories of the author's 1881 edition plus Mariano Catalina's biography. Text used for the translation of "The Nail."

Narraciones inverosímiles. Madrid: Librería General de Victoriano Suárez, 1943. Contains all the stories of the author's 1882 edition.

Historietas nacionales. Madrid: Librería General de Victoriano Suárez, 1955. Contains all the stories of the author's 1881 edition. Text used for the translation of "The Foreigner," "The French Sympathizer," "Long Live the Pope!", "The Mayor of Lapeza," "The Guardian Angel," "The Cornet," and "The Orderly."

Obras completas. 3ª ed. Madrid: Fax, 1968.

Novelas completas. Madrid: Aguilar, 1974.

La comendadora, el clavo y otros cuentos [El extranjero, La mujer alta, El amigo de la muerte]. Ed. Laura de los Ríos. Madrid: Cátedra, 1975.

Cuentos. Ed. Joan Estruch. Barcelona: Ediciones Vicens-Vives, 1991. ["El carbonero alcalde," "El clavo," "La buenaventura," "El extranjero," "La mujer alta," La comendadora," "La corneta de llaves"]

Los relatos. Ed. Mª Dolores Royo Latorre. Salamanca: Universidad de Extremadura, 1994. An admirable effort. A collection of the complete stories replete in textual variations, notes, and commentary.

English Translations of Alarcón's Short Stories Not Included in this Volume:

Moors and Christians and Other Tales. Translated by Mary J. Serrano. New York: Cassell, 1891. (In addition to "The Guardian Angel," "The Cornet," and "The Orderly": "A Year in Spitzbergen," "The Gypsy's Prophecy," "A Fine Haul," "Saint and Genius," "The Account Book," "Moors and Christians," and "Black Eyes.")

"The Prophecy." In *Tales from the Italian and Spanish*, anon. trans. New York: Review of Reviews, 1920.

"A Year in Exile [Spitzbergen]." Translated by F. W. Fosa. *Golden Book* 12 (1930): 81–86.

Tales from the Spanish. Translated by Mary J. Serrano, Alberta Gore Cuthbert, and George F. Duyster. Allentown, Pa.: Story Classics, 1948. Translations "extensively revised and corrected" by Rafael A. Soto. (In addition to "The Nail," "The Patriot Traitor" [i.e., "The French Sympathizer"], and "The Cornet Player": "A Fine Haul," "The Account Book," "The Gypsy's Prophecy," "Moors and Christians," and "The Tall Woman.")

"The Stub Book." Translated by Morris Rosenblum. In *Stories from Many Lands*, edited by Morris Rosenblum. New York: Oxford, 1955.

"The Nun." Translated by Martin Nozick. In *Great Spanish Short Stories*, edited by Angel Flores. New York: Dell Publishing Co., 1962.

Included in this Volume:

"The Alcalde Who Was a Charcoal-Burner." Translated by Jean Raymond Bidwell. *Living Age* 223 (1899): 514–20.

"The Nail." Rafael A. Soto's revision of the George F. Duyster translation in *Tales from the Spanish*, above. (Liberally augmented by sentences and phrases nowhere found in the original, with, on the other hand, numerous omissions of original sentences.)

"Where the Nail Pierced." In *Tales from the Italian and Spanish*, anon. trans. New York: Review of Reviews, 1920. (Numerous omissions; alteration of chapter format as well as chapter headings; considerable license [e.g., Ch.VII is expunged and condensed into two sentences]; and the ending is an exercise in unbridled imagination, not a faithful translation of the original. An altogether unreliable rendition of Alarcón's story.)

"The French Sympathizer." Translated by Robert M. Fedorchek. *Connecticut Review* 15 (1993): 35–40.

Secondary Sources

Alborg, Juan Luis. *Historia de la literatura española/realismo y naturalismo, La novela, parte primera: Fernán Caballero-Alarcón-Pereda.* Tomo V/1. Madrid: Editorial Gredos, 1996. (Short stories and short novels, 518–26.)

Baquero Goyanes, Mariano. *El cuento español en el siglo XIX.* Madrid: Consejo Superior de Investigaciones Científicas, 1949.

———. *El cuento español: del romanticismo al realismo.* Edición revisada por Ana L. Baquero Escudero. Madrid: Consejo Superior de Investigaciones Científicas, 1992.

Catalina, Mariano. "Biografía de don Pedro Antonio de Alarcón" in Alarcón, *Cuentos amatorios* (Librería General de Victoriano Suárez, 1943) and *Obras completas* (Fax, 1968), under 20th Century Collections, above.

DeCoster, Cyrus. *Pedro Antonio de Alarcón.* Boston: Twayne, 1979. (Only book-length study in English of Alarcón's life and works.)

———, ed. *Obras olvidadas [de Alarcón].* Potomac: Studia Humanitas, 1984. Madrid: Porrúa Turanzas, 1984.

Estruch, Joan. Introduction to Pedro Antonio de Alarcón, *Cuentos.* Barcelona: Ediciones Vicens-Vives, 1991.

Leguen, Brigitte. *Estructuras narrativas en los cuentos de Alarcón.* Madrid: U.N.E.D., 1988.

Montes Huidobro, Matías. "Sencillez arquitectónica y aderezos estilísticos utilizados por Pedro Antonio de Alarcón." *Hispanófila* 34 (1968): 45–57.

Montesinos, José F. *Pedro Antonio de Alarcón.* Madrid: Editorial Castalia, 1977.

Ocano, Armando. *Alarcón.* Madrid: EPESA, 1970. (Biography.)

Pardo Bazán, Emilia. *Alarcón: estudio biográfico.* Madrid: Imprenta de la Compañía de Impresores y Libreros, n. d. [189–?]

Pardo Canalis, Enrique. *Pedro Antonio de Alarcón.* Madrid: Compañía Bibliográfica Española, 1965.

Quinn, David. "An Ironic Reading of Pedro Antonio de Alarcón's 'La última calaverada.'" *Symposium* 31 (1977): 346–56.

Ríos, Laura de los. Introduction to Pedro Antonio de Alarcón, *La comendadora, El clavo y otros cuentos.* 8ed. Madrid: Cátedra, 1991, 11–102.

Romano, Julio [González y Rodríguez de la Peña, Hipólito]. *Pedro Antonio de Alarcón, el novelista romántico.* Madrid: Espasa-Calpe, 1933.

Royo Latorre, Mª Dolores. "Alarcón en sus relatos: el problema de la originalidad creadora." *Insula* 46/535 (July 1991): 13–15. (Special Alarcón issue.)

———. "Sobre la datación alarconiana de 'La belleza ideal.'" *RILCE/Revista de filología hispánica* 8 (1992): 286–94.

———. Introduction to Pedro Antonio de Alarcón, *Los relatos.* Salamanca: Universidad de Extremadura, 1994, 15–87.

Smieja, Florian. "Pedro Antonio de Alarcón's *El extranjero:* Some Aspects of the Historical Background." *Hispanic Review* 37 (1969): 370–74.